The Dreams of Gerontius

Michael Easterling

Other books by Michael Easterling

The Water at the End of the World

Christmas Eve on the Underground Railroad
and Other Christmas Stories

Sweet Hope: an Appalachian Ghost Story

Jasper

Ramblin' Red

Copyright © 2021 Michael Easterling
All rights reserved.
ISBN: 978-1-7344339-1-3

 VALLEY OAK PUBLICATIONS

to Dorian, Theodore, and Shadow

· Gerontius ·

Humans have this little saying: dogs have masters, cats have staff. Cute.

Nonsense, of course, but still, cute.

What it fails to mention is that, besides masters, dogs also have fleas, bad breath, and brains not much bigger than nuggets of Puppy Chow. That humans have truck with dogs is proof that they rarely act in their own best interest, for what does a man gain by a dog's slavish devotion but a tongue-lolling slobberer who eats turds, farts and humps pillows, usually in that order?

Pardon me. My wit, such as I have, is not my most attractive feature. I fear wit, for I have long observed that those who possess it are often of a shallow nature. But if you'd ever suffered a bitten tail, or been forced to spend the night in a thorny locust tree, you'd hesitate before singing the praises of man's supposed best friend.

To be fair, there may be one or two among the general canine population who might be deemed noble of spirit, if not exactly facile of mind, and by their example men may be taught such virtues as loyalty, courage and self-sacrifice.

But is teaching by example enough? A glimpse of the day's headlines is proof sufficient that despite acts of noble behavior to guide him, man has made scant progress toward getting back to the Garden. No, trying to teach by example is like a shepherd crossing a swollen stream, expecting his flock will follow right along. Man doesn't change of his own volition. He must be nudged, prodded, even shoved. Sometimes very hard.

The other half of the expression—that cats have staff—gives the impression that we lug around clipboards, checking off that nails are clean, shoes suitably shined, and time cards punched. Now, I realize man needs his little quips to cajole himself along life's troubled highway; you'd expect a well-developed sense of humor in a species that cannot purr. Yet I find this bit about "masters" and "staff" not to my taste, for the relationship of cat and man is ever so much more than some feudal arrangement.

Haven't you ever noticed that when married couples decide to sever the tie that binds they'll amicably divvy up the accumulated spoils then come to blows over who gets custody of ol' Puss? There's a reason for this that has little to do with a shared reluctance to part with a furry lap warmer, a reason that, sad to say, is rarely understood by the couples themselves. The fact is, a man is incomplete without a cat. Oh, sure, he muddles along well enough with the basic subsistence stuff, but anything past that and he must have a cat, for we are the dreamers for those who cannot dream, the seers for those whose vision rarely rises above the ground.

What, you say, man unable to dream?

Well, no, not really. Granted, he gleans bits and pieces of dream matter, and sometimes even gets a look into the fertile realm of the subconscious, but it is rarely more than a peek.

The problem is, dreams are not the province of those who dabble in sleep, and man, with his pitiful seven to eight hours of sleep each night, can hardly expect to enter dreamland via the freeway. No, to truly dream requires a commitment to the time-consuming business of sleeping, a pursuit best suited to cats, for we sleep longer and dream more than any member of the animal kingdom. If you do not believe me, look it up.

Better yet, consult Freud. It was Sigmund who said, "Time spent with cats is never wasted." That's because he knew of our superior capacity for dreaming. I knew Julia, his house-mate. Sigmund would stare at her hour after hour, the most wistful look in his eye. She could almost hear the cogs whirring about in that great mind of his. *How can*

I unlock the secrets of the cat psyche? How can I access that treasure-trove of awareness hidden within that noble mind?

Of course, cats, like most sensitive creatures, do not like to be stared at, and it was doubly disconcerting when the starer had a reputation for performing vivisections in the spirit of scientific discovery. Fortunately, Sigmund contented himself with piecing together his theories of the subconscious based upon the scant pickings gleaned from his patients' dreams, which explains why his theories were shot full of holes. His mistake was to bar Julia from his bedroom and from his study where he took his afternoon nap, sitting upright in an overstuffed chair. How much more fruitful would have been his speculations had he allowed my friend to cuddle up beside him and lay her head upon his soft beard. Beards, particularly long ones, make delightful pillows. I once had the pleasure of sleeping upon a beard redolent of pipe smoke and salted fish.

Yet almost as comfortable is the pillow Michael sleeps on. Michael, by the way, is an aspiring singer who happens to be my current assignment. When Michael lies upon his side, I curl up in the nape of his neck, resting my head against his. Oh, what a busy, buzzy brain he has, even in sleep! So, I begin to purr, a deep-throated purr that vibrates my whole body and soothes that fevered brain of his. Then, as Michael sinks deeper and deeper beneath Oblivion's waters, my purr softens, until having settled him down into untroubled sleep, I wrap and swathe him round in dreams.

· Michael ·

"Serena, listen to me. I didn't mean to kick him, honest!"

"How can you say that? Look at him. Feel him!" Serena, cradling the cat in her arms, stepped forward. "He's trembling all over."

Michael rubbed his forehead. "Look, you've got to believe me, I love that cat, I do. It's just ... look, mind if I sit down? I've had a helluva night."

Though angry, Serena didn't begrudge Michael a chair. He sat, leaning forward, elbows resting on his knees. "All right, I kicked him. I admit it. But you've got to believe I love Gerry-cat. It's just that sometimes he absolutely drives me up the walls."

"Gerry-cat?"

"Yeah, that's kind of my nickname for him. His real name is Gerontius from *The Dream of Gerontius* by Edward Elgar, my absolute, all-time favorite oratorio."

"I can believe that," Serena said. "I could tell by the way you sang tonight."

Michael sat up tall. "You were there?"

"No, but I was listening to you on the college radio station. You were wonderful."

"Thank you, I ... Christ!" Michael leaned forward and buried his head in his hands.

Serena was starting to soften toward Michael and his rollercoaster emotions. "Look, would you like a cup of tea?"

Michael lifted his head. "You don't mind? I mean, I'm sorry to trouble you this late, but I couldn't find Gerontius anywhere, and I know he sometimes comes to visit you."

"It's okay. I'm usually up late anyway, weaving."

Michael smiled. "I know." He pointed to Serena's loom pushed against the wall. "Thump, thump, thump. I can hear it reverberating down through the walls."

"Sorry," she said.

"Why sorry? If you can put up with me and my voice students, I can certainly tolerate a little thumping."

"I'll go put the kettle on." But as Serena started to hand Gerontius to Michael, Gerontius mewed piteously.

"Oh, Gerry-cat!" Michael exclaimed. "What have I done?"

"Look," Serena said, "let me set him on the window seat. He'll be more comfortable there." She gently placed Gerontius on the window seat cushion then partially draped a throw over him. "You know, cats have very fragile organs. First thing tomorrow, you should take him to a vet."

"I will," Michael said, scratching Gerontius behind an ear. "God, listen to him. He's actually purring. I abuse him, and he still likes me." Michael tucked the throw more snugly around Gerontius before following Serena into the kitchen. "I don't suppose you have anything stronger than tea? A beer, maybe."

"Sorry, just tea." Serena lit the burner and placed the kettle upon it. "Why Gerontius?"

"You mean why did I name him Gerontius, or why do I love the oratorio so much?"

"Both."

"Well, *The Dream of Gerontius* is a work of heart-breaking beauty, and the place where I got Gerontius, the city animal shelter, is a place that's just plain heart breaking." Michael pulled out a chair from under the small kitchen table and sat down. "I don't know if you've ever been there, but they've got this big room crammed floor to ceiling with cages. They've some really nice cats, but it's obvious a lot of them are wild, and I was looking for a nice friendly cat that was used to being around people. Then I came to the cage Gerontius was in. I knew right off there was something special about him. I mean, most of the other cats if they weren't spitting at me were kind of lifeless, like they were already resigned to the fact that, pretty soon, they were going to be put down. But Gerry-cat was bright-eyed and bushy-tailed, and incredibly friendly, a real people cat. He stuck his paw right out through the cage just like he wanted to shake hands.

"Of course, I was immediately taken by him, but I still wanted to look around and check out the other cats. But when I leaned over to look at the cat in the cage underneath, Gerry-cat reached down and started poking me in the head, like he was saying, 'Hey, you gotta learning disability or something? I'm your cat, that's it, end of discussion. Now, take me home.' " Michael laughed. "I went to the animal shelter to choose a cat, but it was more like the cat chose me."

Serena lifted the kettle off the burner and poured boiling water into two cups, followed by tea bags. "And you named him after a piece of music?"

"Well, yes and no. It's just that when I was holding him for the first time, listening to him purr, a little voice said, 'Gerontius.' You know, I'm not exactly what you'd call a believer or anything, but sometimes it really feels like fate brought us together, only if that's the case, then fate's sure got a really twisted sense of humor."

"How do you mean?"

Michael blew on his tea to cool it. "I'm afraid it would take too long to explain."

"That's alright; it's Friday night, no work tomorrow."

Michael set his cup down on the table. "Okay, but if I'm going to tell the whole thing, I'm going to need some cookies or something for fortification."

· Gerontius ·

Bright-eyed and bushy-tailed, indeed! For two whole days, I'd been in that horrid "animal shelter" as you call it, waiting for you, Michael. Two days in the company of my miserable companions. Two days of stale dry food and tepid water in a bowl that smelled as if the last occupant had used it for a litter box. Two days of that, and I was ready to tear the cage apart.

Finally, you showed up. "That's him!" I said. "He's the one!" Then you passed me by with no more than a shake of my paw. I couldn't believe it! "Hey!" I cried, jabbing you in the head. "What's the matter with you? I'm the reason you are here. Isn't that obvious? Can't you tell?"

But self-awareness has never been your strong suit, Michael. Even now as I lie here listening to you, I can tell you have no idea that Serena, your upstairs neighbor, is someone well suited to you, someone whose serenity would balance your passion.

Serena. From the Latin for serene, and her parents could not have picked a more appropriate name. Her serenity has certainly calmed you down, Michael. I just hope you do not make a pig of yourself on those cookies I see she is making, because too much sugar always makes you sleepy, and I'm anxious to hear about Fate's twisted sense of humor.

· Michael ·

"I guess I'll have to first start by telling you a little something about myself. I told you I'm not much of a believer, not in the religious sense. But in the last year, I've been having these really vivid dreams, and they've got me to thinking. The thing is, I think these dreams started about the same time I got Gerontius from the animal shelter."

"Can I interrupt for a moment? Would you like raisins in your cookies?"

"Raisins would be great, and chocolate chips if you have any. But no walnuts! I'm allergic to walnuts–make my throat all scratchy. I once had this wedding gig and had this salad beforehand, only I didn't know it had walnuts in it. The absolute worst performance of my life! It was the first and, hopefully, the last time O *Promise Me* was sung by a rusty drill press."

"So you don't ordinarily have vivid dreams?" Serena said, rummaging in the cupboard for chocolate chips.

"No, I rarely dream at all. I mean, I have lots of dreams in the sense of things I'd like to achieve in life, but usually when my head hits the pillow, I'm down for the count, and I can't remember anything when I come to."

"So, what do you dream of achieving?"

Michael leaned back in his chair. "Interesting you should ask, because I think that's something else that started to change about the time I got Gerry-cat. I mean, all my life I've wanted to be a great singer."

"I thought you sounded pretty great tonight."

"Thank you, but I'm not a great singer, and I think I'm finally coming to realize I'm never going to be one."

"Is that why you kicked Gerontius, because you were taking out your disappointment on him?"

"God, no! I kicked Gerontius because he ruined my chance to sing in Carnegie Hall. I don't know if they mentioned it on the radio, but this year marks the hundredth anniversary of the premiere of *The Dream of Gerontius*, and Marshall Banks, who you heard conducting tonight, has been going around to different universities doing *Gerontius* concerts with different college choirs. Come October, he's taking the three best soloists from those choirs to Carnegie Hall to perform in a special anniversary concert.

"And up until yesterday, I was the one Marshall wanted for the part of Gerontius." Michael sighed. "Carnegie Hall! The most prestigious concert hall in the world, only now instead of me making my New York debut, I'll be stuck in my apartment, trying to convince some third-rate prima donna she's still singing flat. To add insult to injury, Marshall has chosen Peter Perloff for the part of the priest. Can you believe it? Goddamn Pete Perloff! I mean, the guy's vocal folds are up his nose." Michael rested his forehead on the table. "And now Pete's going to New York, and I'm going nowhere." He softly banged his head on the table. "Pete Perloff! I can't believe it."

Throughout this tirade, Serena had been methodically stirring the cookie batter. Now she spooned batter onto the baking pan. "Maybe you'll get a chance to sing in Carnegie Hall another time."

"Hah!"

"Look, I'm sorry if you lost the chance, but what does that have to do with Gerontius? He's just a cat, after all."

Michael looked up. "Just a cat? He's more like this jealous, paranoid, schizo ... devil!"

Serena abruptly turned her back, and shoved the pan of cookies into the oven.

"Look, Serena, I'm not the type to go around making excuses for my failures, but my getting that part was a given. I mean, Marshall and

I'd been working on my using this particular register in my voice specifically for the Carnegie Hall performance. Hell, the man's practically been living in my apartment!

"Then yesterday, out of the blue, Gerontius up and attacks Marshall for absolutely no reason. Practically bit his hand off, his conducting hand no less. Marshall had to go get a tetanus shot, and since then, his whole attitude toward me has changed. I was hoping maybe he'd get over it, but tonight at the end of the concert when everyone was applauding, he didn't even single me out for credit. And I was the goddamn lead vocalist!"

"So you came home and took out your frustration by kicking Gerontius."

Michael, looking ashamed, hung his head.

"This Marshall Banks, are you sure Gerontius attacked him for no reason?"

Michael looked up. "Absolutely! And that wasn't the first time he's attacked somebody. In fact, Gerontius attacked one of my students on the very day I brought him home, and I can guarantee Judy hadn't done a thing to provoke him. She wasn't even in the same room as Gerontius. He just snuck up on her and bit her."

"How bad?"

"Well, nothing like what he did to Marshall, but bad enough that Judy hasn't been back."

"If all this is true, I'm surprised you didn't take Gerontius back to the animal shelter."

"Don't think I wasn't tempted. But that night, after he bit Judy, I woke up, and there he was curled up right beside my head, purring. I guess I'm a sucker for a cat that purrs, and Gerry-cat is the All-Star of cat purrers. He's like a little motor. So, I decided I'd go ahead and keep him."

Michael drummed his fingers on the table top. "You know, I think that was the same night I had my first vivid dream."

"So, tell me about it."

"Can I have some more hot water first?"

· Gerontius ·

Really, Michael, if you're going to cast me as the villain in your story, at least me do me justice by telling the whole of it. Judy was not just your student, and don't think Serena doesn't suspect otherwise. You really should pull your bed out from the wall because Serena's loom isn't the only thing that sets the walls to thump, thump, thumping.

From the moment Judy walked through your door, I knew her attraction for you was strictly physical. She didn't even have the courtesy to acknowledge me, your new housemate, but made straight to your bedroom.

For the record, I'm hardly a prude, though I haven't been able to muster much interest in sex since some human in his infinite wisdom decided I should be castrated. But the truth is, in a former life, I was a member of a fashionable caternity of rooftop tomcats who met and with the benefit of cat-punch to lubricate our vocal cords wooed fair felines with our impassioned renditions of Italian arias. I don't regret the experience, though a few months of such tomcatting definitely took the gloss off my coat.

Yet my promiscuity had an even worse affect upon my spirit. Don't get me wrong, I'm not talking about feelings of remorse for failing to follow the moral line laid down by some misguided moralist. I'm speaking of something that underlies morality, and as a consequence, directs it. I came to realize that my behavior was a betrayal of my true self. It was a great chain holding me back from a richer, fuller life.

So, was I to sit idly by and let you to lay waste your spirit, Michael? My purpose here is to help you break your chains, to help you find your true self. And if I should happen to have a little fun while doing it, well, so much the better.

I bided my time, sitting outside your bedroom until you and Judy were caught up in your lovemaking. Fortunately for my plan, Judy insisted on being the one on top. Did you know, Michael, that in the throes of passion she wiggles her toes? It's quite adorable, really. Ten little nubbins waving around over the edge of the bed. It brought to mind a nursery rhyme I first heard during the reign of George II. Of course, it's still a favorite with young mothers today: "This little piggy went to the market, this piggy stayed home. This little piggy ..." Well, you know the rest. Personally, I was rather attracted to one of Judy's "goes-to-market" piggies.

But I controlled my infatuation, for in the matter of chain breaking, timing is everything. In this, I was aided by the steady rise in volume of Judy's ecstatic cries. I already guessed she was one of your students, and here she was improvising an *aria di bravura*, all on one syllable: ah, Ah, AH, AH! I waited for the exact moment when her crescendo reached fortissimo, then made a beeline for her big toe and bit it.

I can't quite say that all hell broke loose, but Judy certainly did. She was a Katyusha rocket, roaring off the launch pad. Her immediate target was the instigator of this outrage, but I am well versed in evasive tactics. I regret that left you, Michael, to bear the brunt of Judy's ire. As she hopped about, trying to pull on her jeans and sweater, she fired off a stream of unprintable invective, then clutching her shoes, she ran out the door, slamming it so hard the picture above your bed fell off the wall, just missing your much-astonished head. Little wonder that Judy's performance left you looking like someone who had just walked into the butt end of an I-beam.

But you were quick to rally and came at me with a speed quite surprising for someone whose occupation is chiefly sedentary. I barely made it to the safety of the top of the kitchen cupboard. Up there, your swats were fairly ineffectual, though I was able get in a few of my own.

Then you went for the broom, which I thought unsporting. I bounded off the cupboard via the refrigerator, slipped as I scurried across the kitchen linoleum, and ran out through the clever little opening you fashioned so I could visit the litter box on the fire escape. No doubt you would have continued your pursuit had you a stitch of clothing on.

As I sat catching my breath, I reflected on the impression I must have made my first day on the job. I hoped I had not overdone it. I knew I dare not go back into the apartment until you'd had time to calm down. In the meantime, I inspected my new surroundings from my fifth-floor vantage point. Across from the parking lot was a community garden, which I marked as a likely spot for catching gophers. Five flights below, the fire escape ended next to a wall that enclosed a small yard that benefited the ground-floor tenant. The backdoor light revealed a little rat terrier sitting on his haunches and occasionally making a snap at moths attracted to the light. Looking up, I saw the fire escape ended at the base of a steel ladder that provided access to the roof. I've never been much for ladders; it is not the going up that bothers me, but the getting down. Still, I've always enjoyed the unconfined space rooftops afford and planned to venture up as soon as I discovered an alternate means of descent.

I was interrupted in my observations by you banging away at the piano and bellowing out *Se vuol ballare*, Figaro's revenge aria, which I took as a sign that all was far from forgiven, and that I had best wait until bedtime before venturing back inside. To amuse myself, I practiced dropping things on the rat terrier and succeeded in hitting him on the head with a turd from my litter box. Of course, he ate it.

Finally, I did what any sensible cat does when bored: I slept and did not stir until awoken by the moon peeking over the edge of the roof. I did a few limbering stretches before stealing back into the apartment and on to the foot of your bed. Tension lines marked your forehead as you slept, and once in a while you would mumble something into your pillow.

I regretted that my actions were the likely cause of your troubled sleep, which begged the question by what right had I to ruin your pleasure? Trust me, Michael, I'm not unsympathetic to a young man's passion, for I still have fond memories of my old caternity days. Yet in my case, I rather think I derived more pleasure from the cat-punch than I did from any amount of wooing. Under the influence of soused herring, I felt happier than I have any time before or since.

Yet life is a scale that counterbalances each experience with its opposite. Without cat-punch I went from bliss to despair, from seeming invincibility to knowing wretchedness. Of course, I could've tipped back the scales with more cat-punch, and this I did until after a few months I was but a ghost of myself.

Yet dissipation isn't my fear for you, Michael. My little toe bite with its resulting pyrotechnics was solely designed to wake you up, to get you moving forward, for my intuition told me that your life was going nowhere.

So how does one move forward? How does one change one's life?

I tiptoed to the head of your bed, snuggled down next to your head and began to purr. I started when you awoke, but rather than exacting revenge, you gently stroked my forehead. Then you fell back to sleep, and dreamed.

The Man Who Was Afraid of His Shadow

"Nina!" I called, for what seemed the hundredth time. I couldn't blame my little cat for ignoring me, for she knew I'd no food to give her. Better she should try to hunt herself up a little mouse, though it seemed even the rodents had deserted our accursed land.

"Nina!"

I stepped gingerly amid the brambles and tree branches, brittle dry from the drought, then spied a striped tail just before it disappeared into a thick hedge.

"Nina, come back!" The high hedge proved impenetrable even for so small a girl as myself. I found a spot where some animal had burrowed under the hedge and managed to crawl through.

"Nina, you naughty cat," I said, brushing the dirt from my dress. But Nina was too busy lapping milk from a bowl to heed my scolding. Seeing her quick little tongue splashing the sweet liquid made my head spin, and for a moment I was tempted to get down on all fours and join her, for I had not tasted milk since my father had been forced to butcher the last of our cows. "Nina, where on earth did that milk come from?"

My struggle through the hedge had gained me admission to what once had been a garden, for there were rose bushes, now choked with dead cane, and a neglected apple tree with fruits no bigger than marbles and likely just as hard. Cracked steps disappeared into a vine-covered wall. Looking closer, I glimpsed bits of brick behind the foliage.

"How odd, Nina. This vine has completely overgrown what must be a cottage, though I've never heard of anyone living here in the wildwood." When I reached up to pull some of the vines away, a whole section came crashing down, and I just managed to get out of the way. Frightened, Nina squeezed her way out through the hedge. "Nina!" I cried. "Come back! It's just an old vine."

The fallen vine exposed a window set within the wall, the glass crisscrossed with trails made where the vine had clung. I stood on tiptoe, trying to peer in, but a heavy curtain, faded and tattered, prevented me. When I tried to push open the window, I found it was swollen shut, so I pounded with my fist to loosen the window frame. Then with a violence that rattled the window panes, the curtains were yanked apart, and I found myself staring through the filthy window at the face of a monster!

I don't recall how I got back through the hedge and out of the wildwood. My first inclination upon reaching the safety of home was to tell my parents what I'd seen, but then they would have known I'd been roaming in the wildwood, a place they had repeatedly forbidden me to enter. And with the drought, the failing crops, the livestock perishing for want of pasture, my poor parents had more to worry about than what, despite appearances, was likely just some queer old man angry for my banging on his window. I decided to say nothing and to try to forget what I'd seen.

Only I couldn't forget, and the more I tried, the more I found myself thinking about that face in the window. For certain, it had been fearsome in appearance, being more hair than flesh, but there was something about the eyes that did not square with those of a monster, not that I knew what a monster's eyes looked like, though I imagined they would be filled with evil and menace, with little devils dancing about in pools of black, ready to hurl out pitchforks at the frightened on-looker. The eyes that stared at me through the window had been nothing like that, for they were the saddest eyes I'd ever seen, like those of a wild animal trapped in a cage; worse, like two black tunnels into a soul where all light had gone out. Those eyes made me feel as if this terrible drought that had been visited upon our land with the desperate hunger that had turned friend against friend, neighbor against neighbor, was as nothing compared to the suffering that looked out from those eyes. Surely, I told myself, there must be something I could do to bring a little sunshine into them. The very least would be to tell someone about the face in the window. But if not my parents, whom?

Thomas, I thought. Thomas the Woodcutter who lived at the edge of the wildwood and knew everything about the goings on within it. Likely he already knew about the person whose face I'd seen and could tell me something about him.

The next day, I found Thomas outside his little one-room cottage made of stone, sitting behind his grinding stone, putting an edge to a hoe.

"Well, 'tis little Miss Priscilla," he said, smiling. "What brings you here? Have you some tools need sharpening?"

I pointed toward the heart of the wildwood. "I want to know about the person who lives in that deserted cottage."

The smile left Thomas' face. "Who told you someone lived there?"

"No one. I was looking for my cat Nina, and I found this window."

"Hush! Hush!" said Thomas, looking around to see if anyone was listening, though, in fact, his house was well off the beaten track. "We won't talk of that here. Come inside where we won't be heard."

The inside of his cottage was nearly dark, having but one small window. Thomas lit a candle then motioned for me to sit at a small table. "Can I offer you a cup of tea?" he said.

"Tea would be nice."

The tea, when it came, was weak, as if the tea leaves had been used more than once.

"Now then," Thomas said, sitting across the table from me and cradling his own cup of tea in his hands, "tell me all that you saw."

I told Thomas how I followed Nina through the hedge and about the untended garden I discovered and the vine-covered wall and finally the hideous face I saw in the window.

"I should've trimmed those vines back," he said, once I concluded, "and those roses, too. I should've cared for the place like I once did. Then again, he likes things kept dark." Thomas thought for a moment then leaned forward. "Can you keep a secret, Priscilla?"

I nodded.

"Mind you, this isn't one of your little girl secrets, something you'd titter over with your friends. I'm asking you like you were grown up. I want to know if you can keep a secret, and never tell a living soul as God is your judge."

I crossed my heart. "Yes, sir, I can."

Thomas leaned even closer and struck a crooked finger in my face. "Because if you don't, if it gets out what I'm about to tell you, then something terrible might happen."

I swallowed hard. "I promise. I promise I won't tell another living soul, no matter what."

Thomas leaned back. "A long time ago there was a married couple who never had any children until late in their lives when they were blessed with a baby boy. Now, I don't take with old people having babies. Babies is for young folks. Old folks are too set in their ways, and this couple was more set than most. They were religious folk, which can be a good thing, only they took their religion way too far. They were always going on about sin, about how man is a fallen creature, doomed from the onset with about as must chance of getting into heaven as this candle here has of turning into gold. And they were always pouring their gloom and doom brand of religion into their son's ears."

Thomas took a sip of tea before continuing. "Now, I won't say that all folks are good, but most got more good in them than bad. And there are a few folks, a very few, mind you, who are born saints, and this boy the old couple was blessed with was one of them, and he had no need to be hearing all this fearsome talk about sin and hellfire and the like." Thomas lifted his cup then set it back down. "You know what a saint is, don't you, Priscilla?"

I wasn't sure. "It's somebody who's killed for what he believes?"

Thomas shook his head. "A saint's somebody who's pure and

innocent of heart. That boy—his name's Michael, by the way—Michael didn't need to be hearing all that about sin 'cause it never would have crossed his mind to go sinning anyway. But being innocent and trusting, he never questioned the word of his parents. Neither did he figure he was different than the common sinner they were talking about. No, he took in all that gloom and doom stuff just like he was the worst sinner in the world."

"How do you know he was a saint?"

Thomas made a face. "You needn't take my word. Ask anyone who knew him, not that you'd find more than one or two that still remembers. But the fact is, goodness just seemed to pour out of that boy. You could feel it like it was something alive. That's why folks wanted to be around Michael, for then the world felt like a better place. Troubles didn't seem so troublesome. Aches and pains went away. There was a feeling of hope and love. You just felt happier being near him.

"His parents saw the way folks took to Michael, and I think they hated him for it. I think they thought it was like a slap in the face, this boy bringing such goodness into the world when they were always telling him there's no such thing as goodness this side of heaven.

"So Michael's parents stopped letting him go out, stopped letting him be seen by others. For years, they kept him caged up in that rundown cottage of theirs, twisting his mind, making him feel like he was the very devil himself. I know because I'd see him from time to time. His father would come asking me for firewood when he was too lazy to cut it himself. Stingy he was, too. Wouldn't pay half what it was worth. But I didn't mind 'cause while I was stacking wood up near their house, I'd sometimes chance to see the Michael peeking out of a window when his parents weren't looking. He looked like a ghost he did, skin all pale. Looked worse as he got older, his hair all wild and dirty. But even then, there was something beautiful about him. His skin was always like that of a fair maiden, white and glowing, and he still gave out that sense of goodness. Just to be near Michael warmed my heart."

Thomas took another sip of tea. "I buried his parents when they died. No one came to their funeral, not even the priest. It fell to me to take care of the boy. I tried to get him to come live here with me, but he's deathly afraid to leave the house, says evil will follow him were he to leave, and everyone would suffer for it.

"So I bring him food and water, much as I can–he doesn't eat much. I set it on the front steps. At first, he wouldn't open the door even to me till I caught on he was afraid of the sunlight. Then I took to making my deliveries after the sun had gone down. Now he opens his door, but only just long enough to take in his food and thank me for it. Michael is as timid as a mouse, and I think for someone to make him come outside against his will would likely kill him." Thomas shook his head. " 'Tis a sad, sad story."

"Do you bring him milk?" I said.

Thomas nodded.

"But where do you get milk?"

" 'Tis goat's milk. A goat can eat plants a cow can't. Way things is, folks here should sell off their scrawny cows and try to get themselves some goats." He finished his tea then stood to take away the cups. "Now you understand why you can't tell anyone? Folks would get curious and start coming around the old cottage, making the boy's life more of a misery than it is."

Thomas carried the cups to the sink. "I say, 'boy,' but Michael is now a man of middle age." He set the cups beside the sink then turned to face me. "You know what the name Michael means, don't you?"

I shook my head.

"Means, 'one who is like God.' "

There was little for me to do at home. One of my chores had always been to feed the animals, but nearly all had gone for food. Mostly, I tried to stay out of my parents' way, especially my father's, for his struggle to keep food on the table often made him short-tempered. I spent a lot of time in my room with Nina, dressing her up in doll's clothes when she'd let me, sometimes reading to her from books. But now, I just sat on my bed, staring out the window, thinking about what Thomas had told me.

I wondered if being near to Michael still made a person feel good. I hardly remembered what it was to feel good. It was because of how bad things had gotten. It was the constant gnawing in the belly, and the worry about what would happen when the last of our food ran out. It was seeing fresh graves in the grave yard and wondering how long it would be before death came knocking upon our door.

The only time I felt good was when I was asleep, dreaming. Sometimes I'd wake, not remembering exactly what I'd dreamt, but feeling happy nonetheless. Then it would come into my mind a notion that it was happiness itself that had awakened me, as if happiness was a thing right there in the room with me. I'd sit up in my bed, but of course there'd be no one there, save Nina curled up next to my pillow. I'd tiptoe to the window, thinking I might steal a glimpse of happiness passing by, but outside all would be pitch black. Then the happiness would desert me, leaving me feeling sad and almost wishing that happiness had never come, so awful was its leaving.

No doubt that's why I thought so much about Michael and the way he made folks feel happy, for I longed for happiness—true happiness, not just a teasing moment snatched between waking and sleeping. And not just for me. I wanted see my father smile. I wanted to hear my mother's laughter. I wanted …

I wanted to meet Michael.

We still had some of the grain that had not gone to feed the livestock. From this, my mother made a coarse bread that was our meal, two little slices apiece, sometimes with a bite of egg. At mealtimes, I began to secret away one of my slices of bread—my parents being too caught up in their worries to notice. When I had half a dozen, I bundled them in an old handkerchief, waited until after my exhausted parents had gone to bed then stole away to the wildwood and once more crawled in under the hedges. Like the window, the front door was nearly hidden by vines. I placed my offering upon the brick step, reached through the vine to knock upon the door, then stood back to wait. Eventually, I heard a shuffling of feet.

"Thomas?" a small voice cried. "Thomas, is that you?"

I spoke not a word, but continued to wait. After several minutes, the door opened and a hand reached out through the vines. I say hand, but the fingers looked more like the claws of a great bird, so long and curved were the nails. They scraped upon the brick as they gathered in the bread.

But as the hand began to retreat back through the vines, it suddenly stopped, and I heard a sniffing like that of an animal testing the air. Then the bread was dropped and, as quick as lightning, the door slammed shut, and the latch thrown.

I moved to the steps, gathered up the bread, then knocked again upon the door. "Michael?"

"Whoever you are, please go away!" Michael's voice was like the door hinges, rusty from little use. Then from within, I heard another voice, this one softer. I pushed my head into the tangle of vines, trying to hear what was being said. I thought perhaps Thomas might be inside the cottage with Michael.

I knocked on the door again. "Thomas," I said, "are you in there?"

"Please, go away," Michael cried.

The other voice spoke again, this time more rapidly. I still couldn't make out what it was saying.

"Michael, is there someone in there with you?"

"Go away, please!"

I felt foolish, talking to a tangle of vines. I pulled them apart so I could better see the door. "Michael, listen. Thomas told me about you. He told me what a good person you are."

"No, I'm not! I'm evil, and that's why you must go away now, please!"

"I don't believe you're evil, Michael. Can't you just open the door so I can meet you? I'd like to be your friend."

"No, I can't and no, you can't. Now please, Priscilla, go away!"

The bread fell from my fingers. I yanked more vines away so I could put my mouth right up next to the door. "Michael, how did you know my name?"

I got no response from either of the voices.

"Michael, you said, 'Priscilla.' How did you know it was me?"

Silence.

I was near to tears. I so wanted to meet Michael. I had spent days going without food just so I could. "Michael, if you're a bad person, how come you gave your milk to Nina, my cat? Only a good person would do that."

When after several minutes there was still no reply, I set the slices of bread once more upon the step then turned away. But as I turned to go, I heard the door latch slide behind me. I turned to see that the door was now open.

Suddenly, I had second thoughts. What I was getting myself into? Was Thomas correct? Was I about to enter the house of a saint, or had I coaxed my way into the den of an ogre?

I took a deep breath to help steady my quaking limbs then squeezed through the vines and in through the open door.

"Quick, shut it! Shut it!"

I shut the door and leaned against it. It was so dark, I couldn't see anything. What's more, the stench of the place made my stomach turn. I longed to throw open the windows to let some light in and the stink out.

"Michael?" I said, my hands clutching the door knob. "Michael, it's so dark. I can't see you."

It was the other, softer voice that responded, and this time I could make out the words.

"Merciful Lord, our Father in Heaven, forgive me. Please forgive my sins in thought and deed. Merciful Saints and all those who've gone on before, please pray for me, as we have been taught to pray: 'Our Father who art in heaven…'"

I listened with head bowed. What I thought earlier was a second person speaking was actually Michael using a different voice, this one with none of the creaky harshness he had used to warn me away, but soft like a gentle wind through the leaves of a tree. He recited The Lord's Prayer hurriedly, as by rushing he would more quickly receive forgiveness. Yet how much could a person sin, living alone, shut up in a dark cottage?

"Michael?" I said, upon the prayer's conclusion. "I still can't see you."

Again, the other voice. "Merciful Lord, please forgive me for all my sins, both in word and deed since I last asked you to forgive my sins. Have mercy on this sinner of sinners, O Almighty and Merciful Lord who taught us to pray: 'Our Father who art in Heaven…'"

As Michael galloped once again through The Lord's Prayer, I began to inch away from the door, my arms out before me to fend off any objects. "Michael," I whispered, "where are you?"

It was the raspy voice this time. "I'm here, Priscilla."

"Where's here?" I said, waving my arms.

"To your right, just two steps."

So close! I stood with held breath. Could I feel Michael's goodness? Did being this close make me feel better? All I felt was fear, for now I'd forgotten which way the door was. Yet the thought came to me that I might have to get even closer to Michael if I was going to sense his goodness.

"Michael?" I said, my voice trembling, "Michael, may I touch you?"

He cried out like an animal in pain. "Don't ask such a thing!"

"But why?"

"'Abhor that which is evil!'"

"But you're not evil."

"I am the greatest sinner of all sinners." And then in the other voice: "Merciful Lord, please forgive me for all my sins, both in word and deed, since I last asked you to forgive my sins …" He went on like this, finishing once again with the Lord's Prayer. I confess I was growing weary of all these "forgive me's." "Michael," I said, when he'd once again concluded, "I'm tired. I'd like to sit down." Without waiting for permission, I sat down right there on the hard floor. "Now tell me, how did you know my name?"

I felt the floor give with the weight of Michael sitting down. "I sometimes hear your mother calling you," he said.

"When?"

Michael began to beat out an anxious tattoo on the floor with his long nails.

"When, Michael?"

"At night."

"You go out at night?"

"Only when He is not around."

"Who is He?"

"The Evil One!" Then with even greater speed: "Merciful Lord, please forgive me. Forgive me all my sins, both in word and deed, since I last asked you to forgive me my sins. And forgive all my past sins ..."

I gritted my teeth and waited. "Michael, what do you do when you go out at night?"

"I look through people's windows. I see you when you are asleep."

"You look in my window!"

"Is that wrong? Merciful Lord, please forgive—"

"Enough already! Good grief, Michael, how many sins could you have possibly committed in the last five seconds?"

"I look in while you are sleeping. You look so troubled, it makes me sad. So, I pray for you. I pray for you to have pleasant dreams. Sometimes, I see you wake. You're smiling. You look happy. Then I know that my prayer has been answered. I want you to be happy, Priscilla. I want everyone to be happy. I want—" There was a catch in his voice. "O God! Merciful Lord, our Father in Heaven, please—" Then Michael began to cry.

"Michael," I whispered, "Michael, please don't cry." I reached out and felt the rough cloth of his sleeve, then slid my hand down to touch the soft skin of his hand. Michael took my hand in his, careful not to pinch me with his sharp nails. Then he gave my hand a squeeze.

I've no words to describe what happened, for nothing I have experienced before or since has ever come close. "Oh!" I cried. "Oh!"

It was as if my whole body was suddenly filled with light, though 'light" is not the right word, for I understood what light was, and that which filled me was beyond my understanding. And later. when I had more time to think upon it, I realized it wasn't my body being filled either, for with Michael's squeezing of my hand, I was taken out of my body to be joined with everything from the lowliest insect to the great sweep of the Milky Way, and yet the insect and the Milky Way seemed the same thing, all threads in a great enfolding presence that if I had but one word to describe it would be 'Love.'

This is heaven!

The thought both thrilled and horrified me, for I did not know how I could stay long in such a realm of bliss and not be consumed by it. Yet I never wanted to leave.

"Oh, God," I cried. "I never knew there could be such joy!"

Somehow, I found my way home in the darkness and back into our home without waking my parents. I lay upon my bed with Nina upon my chest, purring, and her purrs resonated with the joy that still vibrated within my body. I only wish I could have shared that feeling with others. Before leaving Michael's cottage, I'd pleaded with him to come home with me, but in response he kept repeating, "The Evil One! The Evil One!" followed by his litany of "forgive me's." I sensed that the Evil One was somehow connected with sunlight. Yet what sense was there in that, since evil comes from darkness, not light?

On my next visit to Michael's cottage, I brought along Nina, who didn't seem to mind the way Michael smelled. In fact, I never heard her purr so loudly. Maybe it was the way Michael used his long fingernails to scratch between her ears, or his telling her over and over what a wonderful cat she was. Likely, she was just like me: happy to be near Michael. And as long as Michael was content to pet Nina, he didn't seem to need to be asking for forgiveness, which gave me the chance to set my plan in motion.

"Michael, I wonder if I might do something for you?"

The Dreams of Gerontius 27

"It's not something bad, is it?"

"Of course not! In fact, it's a good thing. I'd like to cut your hair."

"But why?"

"I thought it would look nice."

Michael moaned. "Merciful Father, please—"

"Stop it, Michael! I'm not asking you to do anything sinful. Didn't your mother ever cut your hair?"

"My mother told me vanity was one of the greatest sins. When it got too long, she cropped my hair next to my skin, sometimes cutting it. It hurt."

"I'm not going to hurt you, Michael, I promise."

Michael did not respond.

"You know, sometimes I cut Nina's hair when she has a tangle I can't comb out."

Again, no response.

"Michael!"

"All right, Priscilla, if it will make you feel better, you can cut my hair."

Make *me* feel better? The idea was to make *him* feel better. Still, I kept my mouth shut, not wanting to say anything that might upset him. And the truth was, cutting Michael's hair did make me feel better. Being close to him, touching him, sent ripples of delight up and down my spine, though nothing to compare with what I had experienced upon my first visit. I only hoped my attentions gave him pleasure also. At least, I'm pretty sure I didn't nick him with the scissors, even though it wasn't easy working in the dark.

"There," I said. "Now, I want you to see how you look. I've brought a mirror and a candle."

"No, Priscilla. No light."

"But aren't you interested in seeing if I've done a good job?" Not waiting for an answer, I lit my candle. But when I held the mirror out to Michael, I saw he was covering his eyes with both hands.

"Just a peek, Michael. I know you don't like the light, but it won't hurt to take a little look at yourself in the mirror. Here, you can hold it."

I gently pulled one of his hands away and placed the mirror in it. After a while, Michael dropped his other hand and brought the mirror before his face. At first, he seemed confused by what he saw. Then he smiled. "I've not seen myself in a very long time. I've changed." He turned his head back and forth before the mirror. "You did a good job cutting my hair."

I thought I'd done a terrible job, but didn't say anything. "Why don't you let me trim your beard while I'm at it." I reached over and took back the mirror.

"It's Him!" Michael shouted. "It's Him! The Evil One!"

"Where?" I cried. I looked where Michael pointed and glimpsed Michael's shadow, large on the wall, just before Michael blew out the candle.

I'd heard of someone being afraid of his own shadow, but had never actually met someone who was. Now I knew why Michael was afraid of light, and I also knew who the Evil One was.

But how was I ever to get Michael to leave his cottage, which is what I was hoping to do, if he was terrified of shadows? Only on the darkest of nights, ones without moonlight or starlight to cast a shadow, had he ever ventured out.

I thought about this problem that night as I lay in bed, not sleeping, the window open wide to catch a breeze.

"Look at that moon," I told Nina, stretched out beside me. The light of a full moon cast shadows on the ceiling. I turned over onto my side and scratched Nina between her ears, her favorite spot. "It's not exactly a night for Michael to be about, is it?" A gust lifted the curtain making a shadow on the wall that looked like a billowing sail. I sat straight up. "Nina! I've just had a great idea!"

"I'd like us to play a game," I said, taking matches and a candle from the pocket of my dress.

"A game?" Michael said.

"It's one I play with my friends. I think you'll find it lots of fun, only I'll have to light the candle."

Michael moaned. "Merciful Lord, please forgive—"

"Oh, hush! Listen, Michael, not all shadows are evil."

"Mine is!"

I wasn't in the mood for debate. I lit the candle. "Now watch." Locking thumbs together, I flapped my fingers, making a shadow on the wall of a flying bird. "Michael, how can you watch if you have your hands over your eyes?"

Michael slowly lowered his hands. "Why, it's a bird!"

"That's right. Now, you try." I showed him how to hold his fingers. He was a quick learner. "Very good!" I said. "Now, try this one." I held up two fingers and made a circle with the others.

"It's a bunny!" Michael exclaimed. This time he needed no help, but quickly made a bunny to join mine on the wall. Then he opened the circle, changing the shape into a dog. "Arf! Arf!"

I laughed as his dog chased after my bunny. "You're really good at this."

Without my help, Michael made a rooster, a turtle, a monkey with a long tail, a peacock, two goats talking to each other. Like a little boy delighted with a new toy, he laughed at each new silhouette.

"Now, see if you can make Nina," I said. Nina had a crooked ear, the result of a fight with a dog. Michael made a perfect shadow of Nina, bent ear and all.

Then his hands began to shake. He covered his face and cried. Between sobs, he spouted his litany. "Merciful Father … Lord in Heaven … forgive my sins … since I last sinned … all my past sins … future sins …"

I'd no idea what brought on this sudden change, but it had something to do with Nina's shadow. I put an arm around his heaving shoulders. "Michael, what is it?"

Michael dropped his hands and stared at the candlelight. "I had a cat once, just a kitten really. I called him Shadow because he was as black as coal." He wiped his runny nose on his sleeve. "But my parents told me cats, especially black ones, were possessed of the devil. They told me I must kill the devil. I didn't want to. I loved Shadow. But my parents told me that if I didn't kill him, I would become possessed myself." He covered his eyes. "Merciful Lord, our Father in Heaven, forgive me my sins …"

I squeezed Michael's shoulders. "Michael, what did you do?"

He sniffed. "I took him out into the woods and crushed his head with a rock!"

I felt sick. That poor kitten! Yet I felt even more sorry for Michael. I studied him as he sat cross-legged, cradling his head in his hands, softly moaning.

"Michael, I want to play another game."

He shook his head. "No more games, Priscilla. They hurt too much."

"Please, Michael, just try. This is a game like when you made the two goats talk to each other, only this time I want you to look at your shadow and talk to him."

"But He is the Evil One!"

"Maybe he isn't so evil, Michael." I looked at Michael's shadow, which was a perfect silhouette of his head, including the tuffs of hair sticking out from my bad haircut. "Maybe he's just … I don't know, maybe he's just lonely."

Michael looked up at his shadow, then quickly away.

"Please try, Michael."

"But what do I say to him?"

"Well, start by saying hello."

Michael half turned and his shadow followed so they were both in profile. "Hello, shadow."

To my surprise, the shadow actually answered back. "Hello, Michael." Of course, the voice was Michael's, only the one he used for his "forgive me's."

"It spoke to me," Michael whispered.

"Yes," I said. "Now, say something else."

Michael scratched the hairs on his chin. "Uh, nice weather we're having."

I poked Michael with my elbow. "No, say something you really mean."

But the shadow spoke first. "Michael," he called. "Michael."

When Michael didn't reply, I poked him again. "Go on, answer him."

"What do you want?" Michael said.

"Why do you hate me, Michael?"

Michael blinked several times. "Because you are the shadow. 'Abhor that which is evil'!"

The shadow shook his head. "I'm only evil because you say so."

"No! You're evil because you *are* evil."

The shadow shrugged his shoulders. "Well, what if I am? Have you no pity?"

"Pity? Why should I pity that which is evil?"

"Because I suffer!" The shadow seemed to grow smaller. "Think, Michael. Think what it's like being me. The only time I come alive is when you let a little light in to get the food Thomas brings you, and even then, I'm just a shadow of myself." The shadow spread his arms out wide. "I want to live, Michael. I want to walk in the sunlight, to stretch out across the fields. I want to stand tall against a tree, to lean over the roof of a house. I want–"

"No!" Michael cried. "I won't let you. You're a liar. You're evil and your wickedness would spread across the land. The fields would all turn brown, the trees would wither and die, the animals would–."

"You mean, everything would be exactly as it is now?" The shadow leaned back. "Look, Michael, I'm not really like that. If you let me out, I promise nothing bad will happen. In fact, wonderful things might come of it."

"How can I believe you?" Michael said, near to tears. "How can I believe something that is evil?"

"Because, Michael, even though you'd never admit it, what I want is exactly what you want, too."

Michael did not reply, but sat rocking back and forth as he stared at his shadow on the wall. I hadn't understood all that had passed between Michael and his shadow. I only knew that the shadow appeared to be someone distinctly different from Michael, and it was rather disturbing to hear the interchange between them.

Eventually, the candle burned itself out, and in a puff of smoke, the shadow on the wall disappeared.

"Come back tomorrow," Michael whispered to me. "Just before sundown."

When I returned the next day, I brought another candle with me, thinking Michael might wish to talk to his shadow again. But when I arrived, I found the cottage door wide open.

I knocked upon the door frame. "Michael?" The curtains of the main room had been drawn and the windows opened. The room still stank, but a breeze brought with it the perfume of the flowers blooming on the vines. I walked into the center of the room. "Michael?"

From the rear of the cottage came footsteps then a person appeared in the hallway, dark against the light. At first, I thought it was Thomas the Woodcutter, but I was wrong. It was Michael, Michael standing with his head held high.

"Michael," I said, "is that really you?" He had bathed. His glossy hair was carefully brushed back, revealing tidy ears. Gone, too, were the long wisps of chin hair. His moth-eaten coat had been replaced with a fisherman's sweater, much too large for him, but clean nonetheless. Best of all, Michael had cut his long fingernails. "Michael, you look so different. You look quite … well, handsome." I instantly regretted my comment, fearing Michael would think himself vain.

But Michael smiled and shoved his hands deep into his trouser pockets. "I thought I'd try to look a little nicer. I don't want to scare anyone when I take my shadow out for a walk."

"Michael! You're going outside!"

He nodded. "I've given it a lot of thought. My shadow made me realize I can't hide from evil, even by living alone in the darkness.

There will always be evil inside me."

"But Michael, I've tried to tell you, you're not evil."

"Don't be silly, Priscilla, all men are evil. That's just our nature. But trying to hide from evil and keep it at bay by praying for forgiveness did not save me from it. All it did was keep me from combating evil the only way I knew how."

"And how is that?"

"By concerning myself with what's good rather than what's bad. My parents used to scold me for trying to be kind. They said I was putting myself above others. In my heart, I never really understood that. I can understand condemning what is evil, but why be angry when someone is trying to do good?"

"I think, Michael, that instead of loving you for being the very special person you are, your parents were jealous of you. By trying to protect you from evil, they committed evil themselves. But don't take my word for it. Ask your shadow."

Michael smiled. "Maybe later. Right now, I'd rather take my shadow out for a walk."

"Are you sure you're ready?"

"No, but if I don't go now, I never will." He reached out for my hand. "Walk with me, Priscilla. It's been so long since I've walked in the sunlight, I'm not sure I can do it alone."

"Of course I'll walk with you, Michael. I'll stay right beside you. Everything will be just fine."

I led Michael through the open door. But once outside, I was at a loss as to how Michael would get through the hedge, big as he was.

Then the hedge began to shake. A section disappeared, and there stood Thomas the Woodcutter. "Now you know my secret passageway," he said. He stepped aside to let us pass. "Looks like you two are off for a walk. Well, it's a lovely evening for it."

"I'd like to stroll through the village," Michael said, "while there's still some daylight left."

"You do that," Thomas said, patting Michael on the shoulder. "It's good to see you out and about, Michael."

The slanting rays light did little to illuminate the dark woods surrounding Michael's cottage. I carefully picked a path through the forest litter until we reached the main road and stood there in the sunlight with our shadows stretched out behind us.

"How are you feeling, Michael?"

Michael breathed deeply through his nose. "I'd forgotten how good sunlight makes things smell."

Still holding Michael's hand, I led him toward the village. Thomas was right. It was a lovely time for a walk. A cool breeze stirred up specks of dust that danced golden in the slanting light. By comparison, the beauty of the dancing motes made the blighted landscape look all the worse.

Then from behind us came a crackling sound, like bits of paper being crumpled. I looked over my shoulder and saw grass spring up from the ground where Michael's lengthy shadow had passed.

"Michael, look!"

Michael did not look, but continued to walk on. His shadow passed over an abandoned orchard, and leaves appeared on the trees, followed by ripe fruit. Birds, sitting on the branches, began to sing.

I couldn't believe what I was seeing. "Michael, you've got to turn around and look!"

But Michael continued to walk straight on. His shadow passed over a dry stream bed, and it became rippling brook. Pastures that had been eaten down to the roots became fields of lush green. Emaciated cows suddenly had udders sagging with the weight of milk. Where Michael's shadow passed over abandoned gardens, lush greenery appeared. Oak trees rained down acorns. Nut trees rained nuts. Sheep grew thick coats of wool. Barren mares were suddenly in foal. Wherever Michael's shadow fell, there was health and fruitfulness and plenty.

"Michael," I said, tugging on his hand, "You really must turn around and look."

Still, Michael walked on.

We reached the outskirts of the village. When Michael's shadow passed over a house, the cracks in the walls disappeared, the sagging roof straightened, flowers bloomed beneath the windows. Robins swooped down to pluck fat worms from lawns of spring green. Sleeping cats woke up and leapt after fat mice. Dogs sprang up and ran in circles, chasing their tails.

But most wonderful of all is what happened when Michael's shadow fell upon the people coming from their houses. They smiled. They laughed. Neighbors who'd barely spoken, stood hugging each other.

"Michael," I cried, "why won't you look? Everything is just like the shadow—"

"Hush, Priscilla, don't tell me."

"But why?"

"Whatever may be happening is not of my making."

"But that's not true! It's your shadow that—"

"Please, Priscilla! My shadow now has its own life. Let me have mine."

I yanked on Michael's hand, making him stop. "But what will you do?"

With his free hand, Michael pointed to a barn that stood out in the center of a field. "Do you think there are any cats living in that barn?"

I knew for a fact there was a mother cat, and I told Michael about the three kittens she was struggling to raise.

"Well, that's it then," he said. "I shall help her raise them, and I shall be Michael, the Great Friend of Cats. And I shall name all the kittens after ..." Michael scratched his chin. "I'll name them all after things that are dark!"

Then with Michael pulling me by the hand, we ran across the field, laughing.

· Michael ·

"My goodness, Michael," Serena said, "That was a very vivid dream!"

"I know. Usually if I dream at all, it's just this big jumble of images, but these dreams I've been having are complete stories, like I'm watching a movie. All I need is a bowl of popcorn. Say, you wouldn't happen to have any popcorn, would you?"

Serena slid her kitchen chair back. "So what do you make of this dream?"

Michael made a small pile of the remaining cookie crumbs on the platter. "I'm not exactly sure." He licked a finger and dipped it into the crumbs. "Not that I haven't thought about it. The one thing that sticks in my craw is all that stuff about evil and sin."

Serena pulled a popcorn popper out of the cupboard. "Is air popped all right?"

"Do you have some butter you can melt over it?"

Serena went to the refrigerator. "So what bothers you about sin?"

Michael grinned. "Nothing, when I'm committing it."

Serena threw a dish towel and hit Michael in the head.

"Nice shot. But seriously, the Michael in my dream was decidedly medieval. I mean, to be so obsessed over sin."

"So, you don't think man is sinful?"

"I think some men sin plenty. But most sins are fairly harmless, and certainly nothing to obsess over."

Serena frowned.

"What?" Michael said.

"So, what's your definition of sin: no harm, no foul?"

"I didn't say that. I just mean that most sins are just the result of being alive. Look, let's say I'm walking across the grass, and I step on a baby bird and squash it. There, I've sinned, I've taken a life. But what if I didn't see the bird? Maybe I didn't even know that I stepped on it. Even if I did, should I obsess over it? Sure, I'd feel bad about it, but that kind of stuff happens all the time. We can hardly step anywhere without killing something."

Serena waited for the air popper to quit before replying. "It sounds to me like you actually agree with the Michael in your dream, that man cannot help but sin, or step on something, as you say."

"In that sense, yes. But what would happen if I had to worry about every single step I took for fear I'd kill something. I never be able to move. Hell, I'd never be able to breathe, because every time I exhaled, I be killing a zillion microbes, that is if my immune system is working the way it should."

Serena put a lump of butter in a saucepan and stared at it as it melted.

"I think I'm starting to understand your silences," Michael said. "You disagree, right?"

"Not about the level of sin you're talking about, but I think you're missing an important point, a couple, in fact."

"Such as?"

"Well, for one, the idea of intent. It seems to me it would hardly be a sin if you stepped on a baby bird without realizing it. I'd call that an accident. To sin is to knowingly commit evil."

"So, I'd have to first see the bird *then* step on it."

"Let's stop talking about dead birds!"

"All right then, so what's your definition of sin?"

"I think I just said it."

"To knowingly commit evil? So, what's evil?"

Serena took the saucepan off the stove and began to drizzle butter over the popcorn. "Well, for starters, the seven deadly sins."

"The seven deadly sins? God, let's see if I remember any of them.

Doc, Sleepy, Grumpy, Bashful ... no, those are the seven deadly dwarves."

"Pride, lust, greed, envy, gluttony, sloth and anger."

"Jesus! What did you do, grow up in a nunnery?"

Serena held the bowl of popcorn over Michael's head, ready to dump it.

"Sorry, sorry. It's just that you rattled those off in like nothing flat."

"The seven deadly sins are worth knowing. They're also well worth thinking about."

"Why? By the way, this popcorn is really good for air popped."

"Why? Answer me this: Who tells you when you've done something wrong?"

"Usually my mother, which is why I try to visit her as little as possible."

"So, you don't have a conscience of your own?"

Michael took an un-popped kernel from between his teeth and flicked it toward the sink. "Yes, Serena, I actually do have a conscience."

"Sorry, I didn't mean it the way it sounded. It's just that nowadays people seem to take pride in sinning. It's like a contest to see who can be the nastiest. You call Michael medieval, but at least in the middle ages, people knew where they stood when it came to sinning. The seven deadly sins were just that, deadly, because they imperiled a person's soul."

"Yeah, and if you didn't toe the line and kiss up to the priest, you'd be damned for eternity, but only after they burned you at the stake first. Lovely system."

"I'm not saying it was a good system. I'm just saying that people had a clear idea of what sin was. The seven deadly sins clearly spelled it out."

"Okay, so let's look at one of the seven deadly sins. Take lust. Correct me if I'm wrong, but doesn't it say somewhere that it's not only a sin to commit adultery, but even to think about committing it? If that's true, then every nineteen-year-old male is sinning on the order of about every thirty seconds. The problem is lust pretty much defines your average male. It's in our chemistry. It's called testosterone, and short of castration, there's damn little we can do about it. You say people in the middle ages were pretty clear about what sin was. Well, I, for one, am glad I didn't live back then, because there's nothing clear about it at all, and I don't want to have to go around believing I'll be damned for eternity just because I've got hormones. Now, if I were to rape someone, or cause them pain in some way, then, yes, that's a sin."

"Okay." Serena said, "so what about another deadly sin? What about anger?"

"God, I knew you were going to bring that up."

"Is anger also driven by hormones?"

"It's driven by frustration and disappointment. At least mine was. Look, don't make me keep apologizing for kicking Gerry-cat. I know it was wrong. I know it might even have been a sin. But haven't you ever had times when you were so angry and frustrated you just wanted to put your fist through a wall?"

"I've always been too timid to do anything so overtly emotional. It comes from growing up in the family where expressing emotions was a definite no-no."

"So, what do you do when you're really pissed?"

"I sulk. I sit and brood. Sometimes, if I'm lucky, I cry."

"I think I'd rather explode outward than inward."

"Yes, but rather than explode at all, I'd rather do what Michael did in your dream."

"Which is?"

"Make peace with the devil."

"Wait a minute! First you're warning me about the seven deadly sins, and now you're telling me to consort with the devil?"

"I didn't say, consort. I said, make peace. There's a big difference. Michael was very definite about calling a spade a spade; his shadow was evil, and he wasn't about to make alliances with anything that was evil. But he also willing to listen to what the shadow had to say, because, after all, the shadow was a part of him, and it was telling him something about himself that he needed to hear."

"Yeah, that he was absolutely neurotic and should have had himself committed."

Serena swept popcorn crumbs off the table. "Oh, right, have yourself committed. That's the modern way of looking at everything. I'm nuts? Better see a shrink. Better go look for answers out there rather than look inside myself."

Michael shook his head. "I rather thought the idea of psychology was to get you to look inside. Besides, from what you said about the way you deal with anger, I get the impression you're already a person that's pretty turned inward. Some of us who are more extroverted need someone to guide us through the inner realm."

"Okay, extrovert, tell me what you thought of your dream."

"First, let me zip down to my apartment for a couple of beers. This popcorn has given me a monstrous thirst."

Serena went to the refrigerator and returned with a beer.

"I thought you said you didn't have any," Michael said.

"I lied."

Michael grinned. "Sinner." He took a big swig then held the cold bottle against the side of his head. "God, that feels good. Now, what was it you wanted to know?"

"Your thoughts about your dream."

"Right. Well, first off, I wasn't necessarily looking for any deep insights. I looked at this dream more from an artistic point of view. I thought it was very creative the way Priscilla got Michael to talk to his shadow by playing a game of shadow puppets. I remember doing that as a kid. I guess I spent a lot of time in my room."

"By choice or as punishment?"

"Both, probably. I also used to spend a lot of time by myself, bumming around on the beach, looking for things. Then when I got back to my room, where I couldn't be seen, I'd act out stories about pirates and buried treasure and all that stuff. I guess I've always had a rather active imagination."

"Because you're the artistic type, which explains why you became a musician."

"Yeah, I guess. But I actually think I became a musician because I wanted to sing beautifully. Which gets me back to what I was saying about the dream. That part about the shadow reminded me of *Don Giovanni*, the final scene where the General's statue speaks. It's pretty obvious that Mozart was writing about himself, and the statue represented his own conscience, which, considering the riotous life he led, was probably filled with guilt."

"He had a dark shadow, you might say."

"But the shadow sure as hell didn't make the pastures green and the streams to flow again. The statue bears Don Giovanni down to hell."

"But only after giving him several chances to repent of his sins, if I remember."

"Which was something he just couldn't bring himself to do." Michael idly rolled the bottom of the beer bottle around on the table.

"Would you like to go into the other room?" Serena said. "The chairs are more comfortable."

"You really don't mind me keeping you up this late?"

"No, I'm enjoying our talk." She stood. "And I'd like to hear some of your other dreams."

"Okay. Just let me finish my beer."

"Bring it with you."

Gerontius

Let me start by setting the record straight: killing a bird is not a sin! But try telling that to the lady on the first floor, the one with the rat terrier. The dog, by the way, is woefully stupid even by dog standards. A typical conversation with him goes like this:

> Me (sitting on top of the fence): Good morning. Uh-oh, I see she's left your water dish out in the sun again.
>
> Yum-Yum (I kid you not, that's his name.): Play fetch? Play fetch? Play fetch?
>
> Me: So, does she let you out much?
>
> Yum-Yum: Play fetch? Play fetch? Play fetch?
>
> Me: Well, if you can ever make it, we're starting a series of rooftop lectures. The first is to be given by one of the cats who hangs out at the university. He's calling it, *Thought or Intuition,* or, *Cat and Dog.*
>
> Yum-Yum: Play fetch? Play fetch? Play fetch?

What can I say? It has to be inbreeding. Yet I once knew a poodle named Ponto who was not only a stimulating conversationalist, but quite a dog about town. He liked to pepper his speech with allusions from Greek mythology, though he was forever scrambling the characters. On the down side, Ponto was also a bit of a practical joker with a rather vulgar trick of sneaking up behind me with a cold nose.

But I have gotten away from my topic, which is the killing of birds. Tired of my one-sided conversation with Yum-Yum, I went to the community garden to hunt for gophers. As luck would have it, there was a flock of mourning doves pecking at fallen sunflower seeds, and I quickly dispatched one of them. Then just as I was about to tuck into breakfast, I thought of poor Yum-Yum penned up in his tiny yard and decided to share my meal with him. But as I was sitting atop the fence, dropping dove innards down to Yum-Yum's waiting mouth, the lady of the house came storming out.

"You vile cat!" she screamed.

I looked over my shoulder, wondering what cat she was referring to. Then she came at me with a broom. I ask you, what is it with humans and brooms? Deciding it would be best to partake of my breakfast in more congenial surroundings, I jumped down off the fence. But it was not the same after that. The dove had cooled and lost much of its savor. On top of that, I ingested too many feathers with the result that I was off my feed for days.

That said, let me make a few comments about your discussion of Michael's dream. I like what you said, Serena, about the seven deadly sins, that they were called deadly because they imperiled one's soul. Of course, talk of imperiled souls conjures up visions of little devils dragging poor sinners down to hell, which was obviously Michael's first reaction and likely the reason behind his associating his dream with *Don Giovanni*.

Let us dispense with the little devils, shall we? The idea behind a soul is really quite simple. The soul is just the core of who we truly are. Imperilment, too, is nothing complex; it means to separate oneself from God, which is to say to be separate from oneself, or separate from one's core values, which is dooming oneself to a half-life.

So, what about you, Michael? You seem to me someone divided from his soul. On one hand, you have your wish: you sing beautifully. Yet I've noticed that singing brings you little joy. Since I've been with you, I've watched as you have clawed and scratched your way up the ladder of your music career. I've seen you take delight in ridiculing your peers and even your betters. I've watched you berate your poor students and make their lives miserable, ostensibly for their lack of discipline, but really because they have had the audacity to share your own dream, though I wonder if you know any longer what that dream is. I think that you, like most humans, are cursed with ambitions that are contrary to your true feelings, that are at war with your soul.

Oh, that you were a cat, for we know what an undivided soul is! It's running up a tree just to be running up a tree. It's a fat gopher between your teeth and the delicious hot blood trickling down your throat. It's lying in the sun when the day is cool or in the shade when the day is hot. It's a soft lap and being petted in just the right spot. It's not having a care in the world, nor a schedule to keep, nor the slightest ambition other than to eat as many birds as digestion will tolerate. For cats are chockful of the sense of the present, and if humans generally do not appreciate the way we …

Excuse me. I do go on. I fear pride is my sin. What's more, it's false pride, for tonight I fail to live up to my boasting. I am afraid Michael's kick has exacerbated a problem I have been having with my kidneys. Lately, I have been retaining too much water. Then again, if you had to use my litter box, which Michael cleans about as often as Yum-Yum discourses on quantum mechanics, then you would put off going until the back pressure was shoving your teeth out.

But what I am trying to tell you, Michael, is that you already cast a long shadow. Now it's up to you to look at it, talk to it, then decide whether you want it to be a green pasture or a statue waiting to drag you down to hell.

· Michael ·

"If I may ask," Michael said, leaning forward on the sofa to take a caramel out of the candy dish on the coffee table, "which of the seven deadly sins are you guilty of?"

"All of them," Serena said, sitting next to Gerontius on the window seat.

"All? Pride, lust ..."

"Pride, lust, greed, envy, gluttony, sloth and anger."

"But that would make you someone on the order of Jack the Ripper."

"Thank you, very much."

"No, I mean it," Michael said. "You can't possibly be guilty of all those sins."

"We all are, Michael. Haven't you ever been guilty of pride? Haven't you lusted after something? Haven't you–"

"Okay, okay. In small ways, I guess I'm guilty of all seven. But let's say you were in a court of law–"

"Or before the court of God."

"Okay, before the court of God. What sin would God find you most guilty of?"

Serena scratched Gerontius between his ears. "That's a hard one, but right off hand, I'd have to say pride."

"Really?"

"Yes. Why? You think my sin is something else?"

"No, it's just that ... well, when I think of someone who's guilty of pride, I think of Marshall Banks, who conducted *The Dreams of*

Gerontius tonight. I mean, the guy's a genius and probably the best choral conductor since Robert Shaw, but he's also got an ego strong enough to power New York City. But you ... I mean, I haven't known you all that long, but I've always thought of you as being kind of quiet and shy and ... well, modest."

"And quiet, shy, modest people can't be proud? Believe me, if you made fun of one of my weavings, you'd see my claws."

"I thought you said you weren't emotional."

"All right, you wouldn't see my claws. But inside, I'd be fuming."

Michael reached for another caramel. "You know, I can't quite see pride as a sin. I mean, we're supposed to be proud, aren't we? We're supposed to take pride in our work, in our appearance; we're supposed to be proud to be Americans. For pride to really be a sin, it would have to be way over the top."

"I think they call that overweening pride."

"Right, overweening pride. Just normal pride is a virtue in my way of thinking."

"And probably most people's way of thinking, but I think you're all wrong." Serena laughed. "There, I told you pride is my worst sin; Serena's right and everyone else is wrong."

"But how can it be wrong to take pride in one's work? I'm proud to be a singer, because let me tell you, singing is not easy, at least it hasn't been for me. It's taken twenty years of hard work to develop this voice."

"I understand. You've worked for it, you're proud of it."

"Don't get me wrong. I don't go around saying I'm the best tenor in the world, but yes, I'm proud of what I've accomplished."

Serena looked down at Gerontius and passed her hand lightly over his back.

"There's that silence again," Michael said.

"Actually, I was just thinking. Let me first say that I see your point; we certainly don't want a world in which no one takes pride in his work; we've got enough of that already. But nowadays you hear a lot of talk about being proud and having self-esteem and striving for excellence and wanting to do your best, and to me it's all so ... I don't know exactly, but it seems ... well, it seems like the sin of pride. It puts the priority upon one's own ambitions. It's all about oneself and nothing about others. How come no one ever says, I want to help someone else to be the best *they* can be, or, I don't care about being the best, I just want to be a good person? I guess what I'm trying to say is, how can you be truly proud of yourself if your focus is just yourself?"

"So, we shouldn't have self-esteem?"

"I didn't—"

"Because I've spent a lot of time feeling bad about myself, and believe me it's not exactly a feeling I enjoy. Nor did it make me the type of person you'd want to be around. So, if pride is a sin, I say, sin on!"

Serena scooted back on the window seat. "Okay, so if we're doing true confession here, what's your worst sin?"

Michael reached for another caramel then decided against it. "Would you believe me if I said, I don't know."

"Don't know or don't want to say."

"Listen, I'm being honest with you. None of the seven deadly sins, at least the ones that I think really *are* a sin, seem to describe my own particular brand of sin. I guess if the seven deadly sins were some kind of moral smorgasbord, and I could pick and choose bits and pieces off each one, then I could probably put together my sin, but I don't know if you could put a name to it."

Michael decided to have another caramel after all. "Look, for some reason, all this talk of sin has got me thinking about another of my dreams. I remember this one was back in February because at the time I was doing a lot of vocal coaching for the City Opera. They were rehearsing Pergolesi's *The Brothers in Love*, which is a fun, lighthearted, comic opera—a real period piece that's perfect in its own way. But this moron of a director had everyone going around keeping journals and writing reams on the inner motivation of their characters, as if they were doing goddamn Tennessee Williams. On top of that, she knew next to nothing about singing. Get this: I once asked her who her favorite singer was, and she said Julio Iglesias. I'm not kidding, goddamn Julio Iglesias."

Michael ran his hands through his hair. "Sorry. I guess you can tell I'm still pissed. But anyway, trying to work with this idiot director was a nightmare. I'd come home, feeling like I'd spent the night being worked over with a pipe wrench. That's when I was glad I didn't take Gerry-cat back to the animal shelter, because, at the time, he seemed to be the only friend I had. I'd lie in bed, not sleeping, and he would curl up beside me on my pillow. Somehow when you've got a cat snuggled up against you, purring, it's easy to forget the 'slings and arrows' and just go to sleep. And that's when I had this dream."

One-Dress Alice

I reckon folks 'round here think me crazy, and likely they're right. I ain't never had me no steady job, not that a steady job means you ain't got a screw loose somewheres, not in this coal town anyways, otherwise ever'body be crazy, and come to think on it, I'm not at all sure they ain't. It's mining that makes them that way, 'cause when they're not risking life and limb down there in the bowels of the earth, they're sitting 'round in the bars, hoping their beer money don't give out before payday. It's a hard life. A hard, ugly life in a hard, ugly town, and there ain't no place in the world I'd rather be.

That's 'cause I see beauty where most don't. Comes from having no job, you see. No job and no roof over my head. Never could abide being indoors. Makes me all feverish and antsy, like being stuck in a cage. I sleep where I can, but mostly in Church Alley 'cause that's where the Methodist minister's wife sometimes leaves a few scraps out for me. Church Alley's about halfway up the Hill, and that's where you'll find beauty come a winter's morning. I snuggle down where the church's boiler vents out and watch as the miners leave for the morning shift. It's still dark out, and each miner carries an oil lamp to light his way. At first, there ain't but one or two, but as the time nears for the whistle to blow, there's a whole string of lights all the way from Cotter's Mercantile up to the wheelhouse, and 'cepting for the crunch of boots on snow, all's quiet, and the whole thing makes me think of monks on their way to morning prayers, for the procession of miners is likewise solemn, and in its own way just as sacred.

One by one the lights disappear and all's dark again. Still, I wait till

I hear the whistle. Then a door bangs open and there's Billy Dean with his oil lamp swinging all crazy as he's running along, trying to get his arms into his jacket, as if running at this stage would keep his pay from being docked. But Billy's ongoing battle with time has got a beauty about it, too.

It was a different sorta beauty I saw when I first set eyes on One-Dress Alice. It was mid-autumn, and I was down by the creek, trying to catch me a fish for breakfast. As I sat, looking down from a branch hanging out over the water, the children came along on their way to school. I've always had a fondness for children, and they've mostly been kind to me, knowing, as ever'body does, I'm harmless. Several sung out a greeting as they skipped along, lunch buckets swinging at the end of spindly arms. When the last of the stragglers passed, I settled into some serious fishing. That's when I saw her, ambling along, sorta off in her own world. She looked no bigger than a button, and with neither lunch bucket nor books to occupy her arms, she stopped to pick leaves off a maple tree. I saw right away there was a purpose to her leaf gathering; only the biggest, brightest colored leaves were suitable for the fan she was making by holding all them pretty leaves by their stems. Then when she come up to where I was sitting, she gathered a fistful of her too long dress, and fanning herself with her leaves, she curtsied right there before me. Yes, kind sir, she said, I would love to dance with you.

I confess to having been addressed in many ways peculiar, but usually not by somebody sober, and never just a slip of a girl. Still, I was game to do my part in this bit of tomfoolery. I nodded my head and bowed as deep as my stiff back would let me. She smiled, then lifting up the hem of her dress, she waltzed in circles along the dusty lane to the schoolhouse.

That's beauty, I told myself, and by beauty I don't mean that One-Dress Alice was pretty, for as to that, I reckon she was about average. Beauty, to my way of thinking, is something akin to spirit, and I could tell right off that One-Dress Alice had more spirit packed into that tiny body of hers than all the town folk put together.

Perhaps it's right here I should explain about that name, One-Dress Alice. The lady folk in our town, 'less they're somebody rich like the mine owner's wife, have but two dresses, one for ever'day and one for Sundays. 'Tain't nothing shameful about this; it's the way of poor women ever'where.

But woe to the girl who owns just one dress, for there's nothing worse than the scorn of them that's poor for them that's even poorer, and poor Alice, daughter of a poor, poor widow, had but one dress.

Now 'cause of me owning nothing but what I wear on my back, I felt a 'mediate kinship with One-Dress Alice, and I set to watching for her as she'd come and go from school, or town, or church, and always in that same outsized dress. Eventually, someone must've slipped her name to Ladies' Aid Society, for one Sunday she showed up at church dressed in a different calico, and this one about the right size. But by then, the name One-Dress Alice had already stuck, and with it came all the shame of being the one deemed beneath all others. I never heard of One-Dress Alice being invited to a dance or picnic, never saw her playing with other children, though I'd often catch her off by herself, acting out some fairytale. Though I enjoyed her little performances, I know most folks reckoned she had a loose screw somewheres. Nobody but me saw her special qualities. Nobody, that is, but Miss Oleaster Brown, the organist at the Methodist church.

When Miss Brown started giving One-Dress Alice piano lessons, folks come right out and asked her why she was wasting her time. They'd hear One-Dress Alice practicing her lessons on the piano in the church recreation hall, and they'd shake their heads and walk away laughing. She's just One-Dress Alice, they said. She'll be the same ragged girl when her fool's dream of being a piano player is through.

Fool's dream or no, I loved to hear her play, and in summer I'd sit on the big stump outside the rec hall, and her notes would come drifting out through the open windows and alight upon my back and shoulders, making my skin go all atingle much like the time I drank some of Luther Calder's fizzy water. Right from the get-go, there was something electrifying about the way One-Dress Alice played. It seemed in finding the piano, she finally found a way to speak her heart.

Winters was harder for me, but I'd lean against the building and put my ear to the crack where the window didn't sit right. The cold air would come down off the roof like an icy shower, but hearing One-Dress Alice play the piano warmed my heart, and when the heart's warm, there's not much that a body can't put up with. I'd see her there through the window all hunched over the piano, trying to read her music by the dim light of a single bulb, and her so tiny and that big upright like a mountain towering over her. But then I noticed that for a slip of a girl, she had mighty long fingers, and I reckon that accounts for why there weren't much she couldn't play.

At first, she learned hymns. I've always been partial to hymns. I reckon for simple music, there's nothing prettier. But she quickly moved on to harder pieces, like dressed up folk songs and sentimental fancies where the piano was made to sound like falling leaves, or rushing water, or some such thing. My tastes being fairly impartial, I loved ever'thing she played.

I remember though when Miss Brown introduced One-Dress Alice to J.S. Bach. I feared right then that she'd met her match. How she labored over a fugue! For weeks, she'd practice little passages over and over, sometimes for hours, trying to work out the kinks. Her struggle was a great source of amusement to the town folk. She'll give up, they said. A girl like her just don't got what it takes to make real music. As if them pumpkin heads could tell real music from a hog's fart! One thing One-Dress Alice never played was the type of hillbilly music that folks in town was so fond of. Had she played some old fiddle tunes, or maybe something made popular by Jimmie Rodgers or Uncle Dave Macon, folks might've warmed to her and not been so apt to make fun. But the music One-Dress Alice liked to play was what most folks called long-haired and uppity.

After several months of hard work, One-Dress Alice finally nailed down that fugue, and from then on out, she was like a locomotive under a full head of steam. Seems like there weren't nothing she couldn't play. Finally, there come a time when Miss Brown hadn't a thing left to teach her. One thing she did though was show One-Dress Alice how to listen to music then play what she was hearing. Miss Brown would put something on the gramophone, and the two of them would listen for a while, then One-Dress Alice would sing and play what she just heard. It was a wonder to me how she did that, 'cause the music often weren't just the piano, but a whole orchestra going full on. Still, when she got it all figured out on the piano, you could actually hear all them different melodies the instruments was playing. She a had nice voice, too; small, like her, but real pretty, and she could sing all them foreign words just like on the records.

One song she'd sing a lot, weren't in no foreign tongue. Even now I can still hear some of the words in my head.

> *I know not what I was playing,*
> *Or what I was dreaming then*
> *But I struck one chord of music,*
> *Like the sound of a great Amen.*
> *It flooded the crimson twilight,*
> *Like the close of an angel's psalm,*
> *And it lay on my fevered spirit*
> *With a touch of infinite calm.*

When she sang that song, I forgot all my aches and pains. I forgot the growl in my empty belly. I forgot that the nights was getting cold, and they'd taken to firing up the church boiler just on weekends. I'd look through the window of the rec hall, and the light from that one bulb seemed to ring 'round One-Dress Alice like a great halo. Then she'd play that angelic music, and it settled on me like silvery beams of heavenly light and soothed my fevered spirit with feelings of infinite calm.

But not so the town folk. Seems the better One-Dress Alice played, the more agitated they got. You see, One-Dress Alice did what she weren't supposed to do: she got above her raising. Them's that are low are supposed to stay low, and One-Dress Alice not only rose up, she rose up in a way that kinda scared folks. They didn't like the music she played, but they also sensed there was something powerful in it, something that maybe if they was a little smarter or a little richer or a little more worldly, they'd likely appreciate. One-Dress Alice made them realize there was a great big old world out there, and compared to that big old world, theirs was like an anthill to a castle, and rather than being the important people they always thought they was, they was just ants.

Boys would stand outside the rec hall and holler: "Play something we know, you goddamned rag doll!" Then they'd throw things through the open window. Once it was a dead skunk. I tried to run them off, but then they turned on me and run *me* off! If it'd been anybody but One-Dress Alice, the parents of them boys sure would've given them what for, but nobody said a word. I reckon that was 'cause them boys was doing what ever'body else was wanting to do, and saying the things they'd like to be saying. Nobody stuck up for One-Dress Alice 'ceptin' Miss Oleaster Brown, and then she died.

From then on, things kinda went from bad to worse for One-Dress Alice. The ladies from the Missionary society started asking why the church was heating a whole building just so one little girl could piddle 'round on the piano when there was heathen out there hungry for the word of God and not enough missionaries to go 'round. So, the church finance committee cut the heat to the rec hall.

That didn't stop One-Dress Alice. She went right on playing, hunched over the piano, a ragged quilt about her shoulders. Still, it couldn't have been much fun. I'd look in through the window and see her blowing on her fingers to warm them.

Next they said they shouldn't be paying for 'lectricity, and that if One-Dress Alice was determined to go on playing, she'd do so in the dark. Unable to see her music, One-Dress Alice sat and played from memory, and her music was more beautiful than ever.

Finally, somebody did what I reckon was the most wicked thing I ever saw. She put a lock on the piano. No one came out and said, "I'm doing this thing." No committee met to take vote on it. No, the lock just appeared one day and nobody owned up to it.

It was 'round twilight when One-Dress Alice discovered that lock. With her quilt wrapped 'round her, she sat down on the piano stool and went to lift the lid, only it wouldn't budge. For a long time, she just sat there without moving. Then her left hand began to play chords atop the piano lid, then her right hand came in with the melody. For a long time, she played like that, with no sound but the pitter-patter of her fingers tapping on the lid. But it weren't the same, and after a while, she stopped, and then she began to cry. Her crying seemed all the more terrible 'cause she hardly made a sound. It seemed that, even in her sorrow, One-Dress Alice needed the piano to express her heart, and now the piano was lost to her.

I watched all this from the back of the rec hall. You see, there's nothing that goes on in this town I don't know about, and when I saw the Methodist minister's wife going toward the rec hall looking kinda sneaky-like, I knew something was up, and I snuck in while she had the door open and hid myself behind some old boxes. It was from my little hidey-hole that I watched her put that lock on the piano. I vowed right then and there I'd never take another scrap from the hand of that awful woman, not even if I was starving to death.

I was still there watching when One-Dress Alice came in later and found the piano locked. Seeing her cry about broke my heart. If I could, I would've busted that lock right off. But all I could do was watch. I watched as she drummed upon the lid. I watched as she cried. Then I watched as she climbed upon the piano stool and tied the chord of the overhead light into a noose.

No! I wanted to cry out. Please! Don't do it! You got no right!

To be honest, it weren't just One-Dress Alice I was thinking about, but myself and how I was going to have to live without her piano playing to warm me on winter nights and make my skin go all atingle and calm my fevered spirit when it most needed calming. But there was more to it than just her music. I already mentioned how beauty is something akin to spirit. Well, One-Dress Alice was the most beautiful person I ever knew 'cause she was the one with the most spirit, and I think some of that spirit must've spilled over onto me, for in seeing all she had to struggle against and just how far she rose above those struggles, I began to see a glimmer of possibilities inside myself, and when you never thought of yourself as amounting to a hill of beans, then a glimmer is like being wrapped 'round in sunlight, and even if I was never to do anything with that glimmer, at least now I knew it was there, and for that I had One-Dress Alice to thank.

So. what kind of a thanks would it be to let her go and hang herself?

I raced out of my hidey-hole and come to a stop right before that piano stool. Then I opened up my mouth and sang like I never sang before or since.

> *I know not what I was playing*
> *Or what I was dreaming then;*
> *But I struck one chord of music,*
> *Like the sound of a great Amen.*
> *It flooded the crimson twilight,*
> *Like the close of an angel's psalm,*
> *And it lay on my fevered spirit*
> *With a touch of infinite calm.*

Eyes wide in amazement, Alice stared at me from her piano stool, but I had remembered me some more words so kept right on singing.

> *It quieted pain and sorrow,*
> *Like love overcoming strife*
> *It seemed the harmonious echo*
> *From our discordant life.*
> *It linked all perplexed meanings*
> *Into one perfect peace,*
> *And trembled away into—*

Alice hefted up a hymn book and flung it at me. "Get outta here, you crazy cat!"

Had she aimed better, she'd likely have taken my head off. Even so, she just missed my noggin by a whisker. I didn't wait 'round to give her a second chance, but ran to the kitchen, used my claws to open a cupboard then squirmed my way out through the gap where the drain pipe went out.

Yet even as I was running and squirming, I could hear One-Dress Alice laughing her head off. She was still laughing when I looked in through the window. I confess her laughter hurt, for my singing had been meant to inspire. Still, I reckon it served its purpose, 'cause after a while she stopped laughing then picked up her folder of music and quit the rec hall.

And that was the last time I ever saw One-Dress Alice.

There's a place atop the Hill where the ore carts tumble their load down off the hillside. Come day's end, I go up there 'cause it, too, is a place of beauty. Darkness comes on, leaving just the twinkle and glow of lights, and I imagine I'm looking down upon a fairytale village, where all the children are safe and well fed; where happy folk greet each other in the streets and fat merchants are obliged to keep their doors open late; a town where there's always music playing and always someone laughing.

Then the fairytale dream is pushed aside by visions of ragged women, hollow-eyed children, and men drinking away their last dollar.

But it comes to me that 'spite of ever'thing, I couldn't have picked me a better place to have lived my life. Like most ever'body here, I've known my share of hard times, but life is made sweeter by the pain one has felt and suffered through, and it ain't as if I hadn't had me my share of joy along with the suffering, and never a day when something of beauty hasn't touched upon my heart.

When One-Dress Alice quit town, rumors flew about what come of her. Somebody heard she got herself a job in Port Arnold, playing in a

Honky-Tonk. Somebody else said she was seen clear over in Loudon, begging in the streets. Then somebody heard she'd been arrested for soliciting. There were worse rumors than that, if you can believe it. But the real shame was that nobody really knew what come of her. Then with one thing and another, folks just kinda forgot about One-Dress Alice.

All 'ceptin' me. I remembered her fan of brightly-colored leaves. I remembered sitting on the stump, listening to her play the piano. I remembered every piece she ever played, and I seemed to hear her music more than when she sat in that cold rec hall with the quilt pulled 'round her. I'd close my eyes and her music would wrap me 'round and carry me aloft till I didn't know where I was, or what I was. Sometimes I'd think myself a bird, which considering the number I've et in my lifetime, seems a possibility. Or maybe it's 'cause I've always thought of One-Dress Alice as a songbird that folks here tried to keep locked up in a cage.

Not long ago, I was up atop the Hill where I more or less live nowadays. The foreman's wife sets a good table, and though she doesn't leave me out scraps, she's careless about putting the lid on the trash can. Her husband gets the big city newspapers, and sometimes while I'm eating, I read what the scraps had been wrapped in. It was one of them times I saw this:

Wondrous Alice

(New York) Returning from her highly acclaimed European tour, the wonderful Alice Conrad Fox performed to a capacity audience last night in Carnegie Hall. Miss Fox has acquired a devoted, one could say, almost fanatical following among admirers of piano virtuosity. Yet it's not just her flawless technique that enthralls, but the passion and power of her playing. Her devotees were not disappointed by last evening's performance and seemed continually on the edge of their seats. Two of Beethoven's piano sonatas, Opus 13 "Pathetique" and Opus 57 "Appassionata" were followed by a brief intermission. Returning to thunderous applause

Miss Fox thrilled the audience with her intelligent rendering of Rachmaninoff's first piano sonata, a piece noted for its technical demands and dark, Faustian tone.

But the highlight of the evening was, without doubt, "West Virginia Reflections," the performer's own composition. It is a hard, gritty work that demands much of the listener. This reviewer confesses that one section sounded more like a cat fight than music. But there were moments of breathtaking beauty, both bitter and sweet, which left the audience practically gasping. The applause that greeted the conclusion of "West Virginia Reflections" went on for well over five minutes. Miss Fox then played two encores, both times waltzes by Chopin. Then to oblige her audience, who refused to let her go, Miss Fox, for her final encore, both played and sang Arthur Sullivan's "The Lost Chord." Miss Fox's singing is not on a level with her playing; nevertheless, hers is a sweet voice and highly affecting. Add the charm of her voice to the mastery of her playing, and it must be said that Alice Conrad Fox is truly Wondrous Alice.

Having read that, I felt like I was no longer of this world, but was someplace where there weren't nothing but a great, golden light and me in the middle of it. Then a little songbird came winging her way up through the light, and I watched until she was just the teeny-tiniest speck. Then the golden glow faded, and there I was, sitting in a rusty trash barrel atop a scrap of greasy newspaper.

But someday soon, I'll be sitting atop the old rubble pile, and I'll look to the sun, which frankly is more smoky-gray here than golden. Still, I'll look into that brightness for as long as I can. I'll look till rivers of tears run down 'long side my nose, and I can't look no more. Then I'll close my eyes, and from somewhere up there where the bright angel dwells, I'll hear the one chord of music that sounds the great Amen. And then, like Wondrous Alice, I, too, will fly away.

· Michael ·

"Oh, my," Serena said, wiping her eyes with the back of her sleeve. "And you dreamt all that?"

Michael nodded.

"And you told it so well, like maybe you've told it to someone before."

"Actually, I liked this dream so much, I wrote it all down. If I ever get ambitious, I might do something with it. I think if I were to add some more characters, it'd make a good opera. I'd have to get a dialect coach to help me with the accents, though."

"But what about the part of the narrator? It's played by a cat."

"It doesn't have to be a cat. It could be some bum living in the street."

"Interesting that cats figured in both your dreams."

"I know, and considering that I didn't start having these dreams until I got Gerry-cat, it's kind of spooky."

"Coincidence?" Serena said.

"Undoubtedly."

Serena stroked Gerontius' head. "Do you hear that, Gerry-cat? Your master refuses to give you credit."

"And you think I should?" Michael said.

"I'll have to tell you about one of my cat-inspired dreams. But first, I'd like to talk about yours. What was that song the cat was singing?"

"You mean, 'The Lost Chord'? It was written by Arthur Sullivan. You've no doubt heard of him."

"He was half of Gilbert and Sullivan, right?"

"The better half, actually. He actually wrote some decent melodies. Too bad they were wasted on those insipid comic operas."

"I happen to like *The Mikado*."

"God, you're got to be kidding. It's trash. I mean, Nanky-Poo? Yum-Yum? Since Gilbert and Sullivan were bent on offending anyone with musical taste, they figured they might as well insult the Japanese while they were at it. And then there's that excruciating scene with The Lord High Executioner. It goes way beyond boring; the absolute surefire cure for insomnia. Did you know the lady on the first floor named her dog Yum-Yum? She's probably a Gilbert and Sullivan fan." Michael, grinning, reached for a caramel from the candy bowl. "You two should get together and subject yourselves to a performance of *The Mikado*. After all, 'misery loves company.'"

Serena grabbed the caramel out of Michael's hand and hurled it at his head.

"Ow!"

"God, that felt good," Serena said. "I didn't brood or sulk, but came right out and showed my anger. You're good for me, Michael."

"But why did you hit me?"

"Why? Don't you ever listen to yourself? I said I liked *The Mikado*, and then you start ripping it to pieces, as if my feelings were of no account. Am I supposed to feel bad because I like something?"

"I wasn't trying to make you feel bad. I was just expressing an opinion."

"There's a difference between thoughtful opinion and malicious ridicule. How come everything with you is 'trash' and 'excruciating'? And what did you call that director you worked with? A moron?"

"Well, she was."

Serena shook her head.

"Listen, you just said you shouldn't be made to feel bad about something you like. Well, am I supposed to feel bad just because I have strong opinions?"

"Did you ever think there might be a human being behind some of your strong opinions? Somebody that might be hurt by what you say? You know, as I was listening to you recounting your dream, I got a pretty strong feeling about what your sin is. Now, after what you just said about *The Mikado*, I'm certain."

"Okay, what is it?"

"I'm not going to tell you."

"Why not?"

"Because I'm too angry."

"Look, Serena, I didn't mean to hurt your feelings. I'm just a person with strong opinions. I've always been that way. I got a lot of passion."

"Always been that way? Are you certain? In my experience, rancor, which is what I think you have, not strong opinions, doesn't come naturally. It takes years to develop."

"So, that's my sin? Being rancorous? That's not one of the seven deadly sins."

"Actually, it is."

"Which one?"

"If you want to know, it will cost you."

"Oh, God! Is this a punishment? Am I going to have to sit and listen to *The Mikado*? If you really want to punish me, make it *Ioanthe*. It absolutely the most awful piece of–"

Serena reached for another caramel to throw.

"All right, all right. What do I have to do?"

"You have to sing 'The Lost Chord' for me."

"What? Now? Here?"

"Why not?"

"For one thing, there should be a piano accompaniment. It's not the same without it. Also, I've not sung it since my undergrad days, and only then to appease my vocal instructor who was friends with this old fart who won some Podunk award for a recording he made of Victoriana. God, I hate Victoriana. It's all affectation and wordy, pompous sentimentality."

Serena moved to get up. "For heaven's sake, Michael, you could've just said no."

Michael threw up a hand. "No! Wait! I'll do it. Just give me a second to see if I can remember the words."

Serena sat back down on the window seat then pulled Gerontius closer to her.

"Be warned, this won't be a great performance. My voice is pretty tired."

Serena stroked Gerontius' head. "Do you hear that Gerry-cat? Excuses, excuses."

Michael stood up. "Okay, here goes:

Seated one day at the organ,
I was weary and ill at ease,
And my fingers wandered idly
Over the noisy keys.

I know not what I was playing,
Or what I was dreaming then
But I struck one chord of music,
Like the sound of a great Amen.

It flooded the crimson twilight,
Like the close of an angel's psalm,
And it lay on my fevered spirit
With a touch of infinite calm.

It quieted pain and sorrow,
Like love overcoming strife
It seemed the harmonious echo
From our discordant life.

It linked all perplexed meanings
Into one perfect peace,
And trembled away into silence
As if it were loath to cease.

I have sought, but I seek it vainly,
That one lost chord divine,
Which came from the soul of the organ,
And entered into mine.

It may be that death's bright angel
Will speak in that chord again,
It may be that only in Heav'n
I shall hear that great Amen.
I shall hear that great Amen!

Michael plopped back down on the couch. "There, I've been suitably punished. Actually, the way I sounded, you probably had the worst of it."

"Why do you say that? You sang beautifully. And for all your disdain of Victoriana, you sang with great feeling."

"Come on, Serena, that's what I've been trained to do. I can sing with feeling even when I'm thinking of taking a crap."

"Nice, Michael, really nice. Why can't you take a compliment? Why must you take what I say and throw it back in my face?"

"I'm not throwing anything. I'm just trying to be honest. Look, what if you were weaving and all the threads got tangled up in a big mess? Then what if I saw it and said, 'Hey! That's great!' Would you sit there and say, 'Well, thank you,' even though you knew it was nothing but an ugly mess? I mean, if you didn't say anything, it'd be like you were lying, or taking something you didn't deserve."

"Michael, you're an absolute wonder. You can twist anything around. You turn arrogance into a virtue."

"So now I'm arrogant as well as rancorous. Listen, Serena, I know what good singing is, and what I just did wasn't good singing."

"Fine. Have it your way. You're the only one that knows anything. Now, for sure, I know what your sin is."

"What?"

Serena crossed her arms and stared at the ceiling.

"Come on, Serena, you promised."

"I know, but if I tell you, you'll get upset, and I don't think I'm up for any more of your tirades."

Michael drummed his fingers on the arm of the couch.

"Oh, all right. It's sloth."

Michael leapt up. "Sloth?" He did half a turn around the sofa, stopped and leaned heavily on the back of it. "Serena, how can you scold me for hurting someone's feelings and then go and insult me like that? Sloth!"

"Michael, please don't be angry."

"I'm not angry, I'm hurt. You've no idea how hard I've worked and the sacrifices I've made, what it's like trying to make a living as a musician, the kind of jobs you have to take just to pay the bills. You don't know what it's like seeing other people going out and having fun while I have to stay in and practice or else go to still another stupid rehearsal. And that's on top of giving lessons all afternoon, which is on top of my own vocal practice, because if I don't exercise my voice, I'll lose everything I've ever worked for."

"Michael, some of the hardest working, most industrious people in the world are guilty of sloth."

Michael released his grip on the sofa. "That makes absolutely no sense."

"On the surface, it doesn't, but if you'd sit down and give me a chance, maybe I can explain."

Michael sat back down and started to unwrap another caramel.

"Instead of sloth, I should've said acedia was your sin, only the word acedia had gone out of use."

Michael popped the caramel into his mouth. "Never heard of it."

"Most people haven't. The word comes from the Latin verb 'acedior,' meaning to be peevish or morose, which suggests a sourness toward life rather than laziness, which is what most people think of when they hear the word sloth. Back in the Middle Ages, people used the word acedia, and it was an affliction that particularly affected monks."

"Christ! The Middle Ages again! What *did* you study in college? Medieval trivia?"

"Actually, I was a history major, but I minored in religious studies. Now, may I go on?"

Michael shrugged then grabbed another caramel.

"Acedia was the sin of monks, especially those monks who lived alone. I think people who are loners are particularly susceptible to acedia. I know I've had to battle it myself. I also suspect that acedia is more prevalent among artists like yourself."

"Why's that?"

"Because artists don't exactly live in the real world."

"I live in the real world, believe me."

"But you don't work a nine-to-five job. You're not married. You don't have children, or at least, I don't think you do."

Michael smiled. "Fatherhood is not one of my sins."

"But all those things serve to ground people. They put them face-to-face with the ordinary problems of life, like making the boss happy, and dealing with sick kids, and saving up for college. Whereas you as a musician are outside those things. I'm not saying you don't have your share of problems, but I suspect your problems are entirely different, as well as your goals. Your goals aren't those of falling in love and raising a family. What was it you said, that you always wanted to sing beautifully?"

"And wanting to sing beautifully makes me slothful?"

"Forget sloth! What I'm saying is that it's made you more susceptible to acedia, because in the normal give and take of life, a person's goals are more modest, are more easily attained. But your goal in life is loftier and much harder to achieve. You said yourself, you don't think you'll ever be a great singer, and think of all the time and effort you've put into becoming one. To not succeed could easily sour you towards life."

"I didn't say I'd never be a great singer. I said I was starting to doubt I'd be one. I haven't given up all hope yet."

"Well, here's the million-dollar question: has your life turned out the way you wanted it to?"

"Has *anyone's* life turned out the way he has wanted it to?"

"You're evading the question."

Michael sank back into the sofa. "Christ, I don't know. It's not something I consciously think about a lot, yet it's always in the back of my mind—wanting to be a great singer, wanting to have the recognition, the chances to perform in major concert halls, to make a lot of money. I've always dreamed of achieving those things, but it's kind of like the carrot stick before the horse. I see it out there, but I just can't seem to grab it. Tell me more about the monks. How come they were more susceptible to acedia?"

"Here, let me read you something."

Serena gently moved Gerontius aside, went to a bookshelf and returned with what looked like a textbook. Sitting back down, she opened the book to a marked page. "This was written by John Cassian, a fourth-century monk."

> When the monk is beset by acedia, he detests the place where he is and loathes his cell; he has a poor and scornful opinion of his brethren near and far, and thinks that they are neglectful and unspiritual. It makes him sluggish and inert for every task, and he cannot sit still nor give his mind to reading. He thinks despondently how little progress he has made where he is, how little good he gains or does—he who might so well direct and help others, and while where he is, has nobody to teach and nobody to edify. He dwells much on the excellence of other and distant monasteries. He thinks how profitable and healthy life is there, how delightful the brethren are, and how spiritually they talk. On the contrary, where he is all seems harsh and untoward, there is no refreshment for his soul to be got from his brethren, and none for his body from the

thankless land.

"Sounds like the monk was depressed." Michael said. "What he needed was a doctor to prescribe him some anti-depressants."

"It sounds like the monk was committing the sin of acedia."

"We've had this little discussion before. You seem down on shrinks."

"I've nothing against psychiatrists, if, as you say, they help you look within yourself. But I definitely disapprove of taking pills in an attempt to cure what is essentially a moral failure."

Michael grinned. "So how does one atone for moral failure? Self-flagellation?"

"Very funny. The hardest part for the person guilty of acedia is realizing he's actually committing it. He assumes he's a victim of circumstances rather than someone with a moral failing. So, the monk would likely need the guidance of someone in his order to help him recognize his sin. Cassian suggested the cure for acedia is prayer and manual labor."

"God, I've always prayed I could avoid manual labor! But seriously, it sounds to me like taking a pill would be a lot easier. And this thing about praying for help assumes you believe in God, or that He even exists."

"Ah! but disbelief doesn't let a sinner off the hook! In fact, it may be a sign that he has succumbed to acedia. You know, some say that acedia is the deadliest of the seven sins because it ultimately leads to a separation of oneself from God."

"So why were monks more susceptible to acedia? Because they believed in God?"

"I think it had to do with the way they lived. Cassian founded an order where the initiate first had to purge himself of all earthly desires. The regimen might have been too demanding for many of them."

"Okay, but I'm still not sure what all this has to do with me. I can guarantee you that purging myself of all earthly desires has never been high on my list of priorities."

"It has to do with your attitude toward life. I don't think I've ever heard you say anything positive about anyone or anything, not unless you qualify it with some added criticism."

"Like I said, I'm honest."

"I don't think you're honest at all, especially with yourself. Tell me, what do you think of 'The Lost Chord'?"

"I think the melody doesn't compliment the lyrics. It sounds like a march, like 'Onward Christian Soldiers', which Sullivan also wrote, by the way."

"What about the words?"

"I know you're going to crucify me for anything I say, but I'll say it anyway: I think the lyrics are utter rot. It's overwrought Victorian sentimentality, so flowery you suffocate in its perfume."

"*You* suffocate in its perfume. I find it moving."

"Oh, come on, Serena! *It flooded the crimson twilight? Trembled away into silence?* It's Victorian melodrama. It's Oliver Twist and Bob Cratchit, and that little puke, Tiny Tim."

"I found it moving because the author obviously spoke from his heart."

"Her heart. The lyrics were written by a woman."

"Okay, her heart. She spoke without shame about something which had a profound affect upon her, something that was deeply mysterious. It was as if, just for a moment, she touched the face of God."

"Yeah, and found it was covered with warts."

"And found something wondrous, something she could never have imagined. Something that actually satisfied that yearning we all feel, that need to be united with something far greater than ourselves."

"And you got all that from *It flooded the crimson twilight?*"

"Tell me, if you're not moved by 'The Lost Chord', what does move you?"

"Well, certainly nothing by Arthur Sullivan. I mean, the guy lived in the time of Debussy and Fauré, and he was still writing chord changes that were already old hat in Bach's time."

"Michael, I ask for something that moves you, and you answer with another of your criticisms. That's classic acedia. Can't you think of anything that moves you?"

Michael waved his hands in the air. "Well, you caught me off guard. But let me think about it, and I'll come up with a dozen things that move me, and not one of them will be insipid pap like 'The Lost Chord.'"

"I'll take 'insipid pap' over most of the recent compositions. I agree that 'The Lost Chord' may be overly sentimental, but at least it has a heartfelt meaning, whereas the compositions you hear nowadays may be very sophisticated, but they don't risk expressing something straight from the heart."

Michael jumped to his feet. "Serena!"

"What? Why are you yelling at me now?"

"No! It's–"

But Michael's warning came too late. Gerontius had already vomited on Serena's lap.

· Gerontius ·

My dear Serena, a thousand, thousand pardons. I don't know what came over me, or in this case, out of me, though it appears it was that off-brand of tuna Michael's been getting at the discount store.

But to disrupt your discussion just when you were making headway against Michael's enormous ego is inexcusable. I see you as his Cassian, his spiritual guide, and I applaud you for keeping him from sidetracking the issues. Don't be afraid to be severe with Michael, for I've learned that to get him to see the light generally requires a flame thrower. Yet it's for his own good, for acedia is such a nasty sin, an intractable selfishness, a smoldering resentment against life itself, which, in Michael's case, has led him to acts of cruelty.

Here's an example from that time he was coaching the members of the City Opera. Often he did his coaching in his apartment, which, for me, was very exciting, for the singers brought with them such a passion for their art. But to Michael, such high spirits just begged to be quashed, using his fail-proof weapon: Superior Knowledge. How sad to see a cast member enter Michael's apartment light of heart only to leave weighed down with self-doubt.

He took particular delight in tormenting a girl named Olivia. Olivia could do nothing right: her breath support was weak, her posture lax, her diction sloppy. She sang flat; she sang too sharp; her timing was off; she sang the wrong notes; her upper register was too shrill.

To be sure, there was an air of indolence about Olivia, and had Michael praised her to the skies, I doubt she would have put any more effort into her singing. She always appeared to be someplace else, perhaps at home with her feet up on the ottoman, her hand deep into a box of bon-bons.

But Olivia's true offense was that God had given her a voice of sublime purity and richness, and when she opened her mouth to sing, roses came out. By comparison, Michael's voice, despite all his years of hard work, lacked the sparkle of this bone-idle girl. No wonder he was spiteful. No wonder he wanted to bring Olivia down. Fate had played one of her tricks upon him, and like all those who fall short of their dreams, Michael suffered.

Let me say it's not acedia to suffer. It's only acedia when in suffering one grows bitter, and in the short time I've known Michael, I've observed his increasing bitterness toward life. In this, he's far from alone, for acedia is the plague our time, and just like the horrible plagues of the past, it's just as deadly–more deadly, for the world grows sick with bitterness, and humans shrug and say, "why should I care, it's always been like this," or worse, strive to make discontent a *cause célèbre* with the opportunity to cast acrimony as a virtue.

But thanks to you, Serena, I've hope for Michael, for by being his Cassian, you can help him to recognize his acedia. Once he does, he will likely see that suffering is the basis of it, and perhaps then he can begin to heal himself.

Speaking of suffering, I fear it's not just the cheap tuna that's making me feel ill. It's said that when one's death approaches, Allah lets a leaf fall from his throne with the person's name written upon it. He then has forty days before his soul must separate from his body. I fear Allah dropped my leaf some time ago. I just pray I have enough time left to finish out this evening, for I enjoy listening to you both. I'm particularly anxious to hear you tell of the dream you mentioned, Serena, for I've a feeling I know which one it is.

• Serena •

"There," Serena said, smoothing out the fabric of the skirt she had changed into, "that's better."

"I'm so sorry, Serena." Michael said, sponging the last trace of the vomit off the window seat. "I'll pay to have your skirt cleaned."

"I'm not worried about the skirt. I'm more worried about Gerontius. I'm afraid he's getting sicker. Maybe we should take him to a vet."

"In the middle of the night? I'll take him tomorrow morning, I promise. He probably threw up because he ate a bird. They always make him sick. There's nothing nicer than coming home to find a regurgitated bird on the carpet." Michael held up the sponge. "What do I do with this?"

"How about we rinse it out in the kitchen sink?" Serena said. "This is an odd thing to say after what just happened, but I'm kind of hungry. Would you like some pancakes?"

"I'd love some."

Michael followed Serena into the kitchen.

"Serena, you wouldn't happen to have real maple syrup, would you?"

"I've something better," Serena said, taking pancake ingredients from the cupboard. "It's called honey-butter syrup. My mom used to make it for us when we'd come home from church on Sunday night. I think it was her way of placating us for having to go to church twice on Sundays."

"Sounds like your family was pretty religious."

"Probably no more than Billy Graham's. Sometimes my parents would drag us off to mid-week prayer meeting. Try explaining to your teacher that you didn't finish your homework because you had to pray."

"Do you still go to church?"

Serena spooned pancake batter on to the skillet. "I only go into a church when it's empty. Have you ever been in the university chapel?"

"I think I've sung in it about a gazillion times. The acoustics are great."

"It also has great architecture, not that I know much about architecture. But it reminds me of pictures I've seen of the great cathedrals of Europe. And the stained glass windows are exquisite." Serena stared at her reflection in the kitchen window. "When I'm sitting in the chapel, and all is quiet, and there's light coming through the windows, I get such a feeling of being uplifted."

"*Love lifted me*," Michael sang, "*love lifted me—*"

"Oh, please!"

"Sorry. That just happens to be about the only hymn I know."

"It's because of hymns like that that I prefer churches without people."

"Hey! I thought *I* was the one supposed to be negative." When Serena didn't respond, Michael left the comfort of a kitchen chair to stand beside her. "I'm sorry. I didn't mean my hymn singing to upset you." He took the spatula from her hand. "Look, why don't you sit down, and I'll finish making the pancakes."

"What is this, atonement?"

Michael grinned. "Yes, and it's damn noble of me since I hate to cook almost as much as listening to *The Mikado*."

Serena tried to take the spatula back, but Michael raised it up above her reach.

"No fair!" she said. "You're too tall."

"Blame it on my Dad. He's six-foot-four."

Serena stood on tip-toe as if trying to get the spatula again, then kissed Michael on the cheek. Michael, startled, dropped the spatula.

"Got it!" Serena said, having caught the spatula before it hit the floor. "Guile can beat height any day."

Michael touched his cheek. "Did you really mean that as a trick, or was there another reason you kissed me?"

Serena smiled. "Maybe it's my way of granting you atonement, providing you don't sing any more of those dreadful hymns."

Michael moved closer to Serena. "Well, I don't know. Being forgiven is rather nice."

Serena gently pushed him away. "Let's take our pancakes in the other room so we can check on Gerontius."

Back in the living room, they sat on opposite ends of the window seat with Gerontius lying between them.

"You know," Michael said, spearing a piece of pancake with his fork, "I'm a bit confused. From what you were saying earlier about the seven deadly sins, I got the impression you're pretty religious. But then you tell me you won't go into a church unless it's empty."

"I wouldn't say, I won't, exactly, it's just that when a preacher opens his mouth, I generally head for the exit."

"Why's that?"

"It has to do with the way I was brought up. My parents were very religious in the go-to-church sense, and when you pair strong convictions with emotional emptiness, you get a religion that's little more than moral strictures, and pretty grim ones at that."

"So are you religious?"

"I'm not sure. I'm not even sure if I know anymore what being religious means. I do think about religious issues a lot, even in my dreams."

"Aha! Is this the cat-induced dream you were telling me about?"

"You still don't believe an animal can influence your dreams, do you?"

"Cats are not conscious creatures."

"I'm not in the mood to argue. I just know that, like you, I had a very vivid dream when Gerry-cat was sitting in my lap on this very window seat."

"When was this?"

"Back in December when you locked him out of your apartment on the coldest night of the year."

"I did not lock him out! I just let him out to use the litter box and forgot to let him back in. December is always a busy month for me. Lots of Christmas music. I had a lot on my mind."

"So the poor miserable creature crept away to find some kind-hearted person willing to give him shelter."

"You're making me feel guilty again."

Serena nudged Michael with her foot. "I'm just giving you a hard time. In a way, I'm glad you forgot to let him back in, because I was feeling in the need of company that night."

"And later on when I came looking for Gerontius, we got to really meet."

Serena smiled. "Yes, that too."

"So, what was this dream you had?"

"First, let me set the scene a little. I was sitting here, finishing a sweater I was knitting for my sister for Christmas. On the radio, they were playing Christmas music sung by a Russian men's choir, which I found a bit heavy, so I was glad to have a cat visit me and lighten the mood. And our little Gerry-cat here seemed happy to have a warm lap to curl up on. He purred so hard, I thought he was going to break his purr box. Anyway, with the music and the warmth of the room and Gerontius' purr, I was lulled to sleep, and that's when I had my dream."

The Three Dowries

Long ago in a Dutch fishing village, nothing stirred save a small kitten exploring a hole in the wall of the house of a sleeping fisherman. The hole did not appear big enough for a mouse, let alone a kitten, but this half-frozen runt was desperate, and the warm, food-scented air emanating from the crack ever so enticing.

Finding the hole more constrictive than her recent passage through her mother's birth canal, she nevertheless wiggled and writhed, squeezed and squirmed, until she got one paw through. Jamming her head alongside, she squiggled and scrunched, but the hole would not admit both arm and head. Still, she was reluctant to withdraw on account of the warm air playing over her icy toes. Relaxing, she purred and kneaded the warm air. Then it was head first, nose forward, pink nostrils flaring, white whiskers flat against the wall. Her forehead was too wide, yet she was a contortionist, and tweaked her head to conform to the shape of the hole. Blue eyes bulged, the skin about the eyes stretching like a heavily laden fish net.

After much thrusting and twisting, she succeeded in getting her head through, and it was here she paused to gather strength. If at that moment the resident of the house had been awake, what a queer sight he would have seen! A head, nothing more, projecting from the wall, the absurd trophy of a very-small-game hunter. Yet, to the kitten, this was no cause for amusement, for now her front legs were pinned and her hind legs so tightly wedged, only the small power of her toes availed her. She gripped and re-gripped the ancient framework until her tiny claws split and the muscles of her feet were racked with fiery spasms. This was a battle between life and death with victory measured by the progress of a hair's thickness! After seeming ages of scratching and squiggling, she managed to get both head and front legs through the hole. Then it was just a matter of a little butt wiggling before she dropped to the floor.

One would have thought that after such a hard-fought battle, a long rest was required, yet such is the resilience of nature's creatures that the kitten was soon on her feet and seeking the source of the room's heat: a coal fire, burned down to glowing embers. The kitten drew as close as she dared then lay Sphinx-like with front legs stretched forward. Delighted by the warm bricks beneath her belly, she began to purr.

How was it that so diminutive a kitten could purr so loudly, loud enough to wake the dead? Yet Kristoph, the sole occupant of the house, did not stir in the chair where he slept. As to this, the empty schnapps bottle explained much, for if Gabriel had chosen that moment to trumpet the second coming, it's doubtful Kristoph could have harkened.

Once the kitten was thoroughly warm, she began to clean her fur, but briefly, for the chalky taste of wall dust recalled her great hunger and, forgoing her bath, she began a search for food. Success in this regard was doubtful, for Kristoph, a man fonder of drink than food, took his supper at the tavern he had acquired in a game of cards.

But the kitten did not know this, and it wouldn't have stopped her if she had. Sniffing her way across the floor, she came to a shoe, and placing forepaws on one side, she peered within. In response to her weight, the shoe rocked like a little boat at sea, which it much resembled, for it was a wooden shoe with a pointed bow and a high stern. The kitten stuck her head inside the toe of the shoe and found it to her liking, just roomy enough to lie curled up in.

It was a temptation. Still, there was that ache in her belly.

Turning away from the shoe, she immediately began an ascent up Kristoph's leg. She had an anxious moment when Kristoph muttered something in his sleep then crossed one leg over the other. The kitten hung on until the motion ceased then scampered onto Kristoph's soft belly. What a pleasure to walk upon this was! She trotted about in a circle then pounced upon a gleaming button.

It was then that she caught the scent, the same that had issued from the hole in the wall. Sniffing, she moved slowly upward until she came to Kristoph's long, flowing beard. Here was the source of the wonderful smell, a heady blend of many exotic odors. Tobacco smoke seemed pretty much everywhere. The heavy smell of lamp oil was strongest lower down where the beard had been used to wipe oily fingers. Stale ale was definitely heaviest around the chin. But the best spot was right in the center of the beard. Here she sat down and inhaled deeply.

Ah, fish!

Of course, being new to the world, she could not have actually identified this or any of the other smells, but that was of no matter. She closed her eyes and purred, kneading the beard with alternating forepaws until she entered into a state of near bliss, a sort of fish-smell-induced delirium.

But better than the smell had to be the taste! Using her raspy tongue, she licked the hairs of the beard only to find the experience unsatisfactory. For one, the hair of the beard was not nice hair, not like her fur. Secondly, though the scent of fish was generally strong, there was little of its taste. Still, the smell of fish assuaged the pain in her belly a little. It was not true food–more like the dream of food–but it was something. Feeling very tired, she curled up upon the beard, closed her eyes, ran her tongue across her pink nose one time, then fell fast asleep.

Not long afterwards, Kristoph began to stir. Perhaps it was the moonlight, now bright through the window, which disturbed his sleep. More likely it was his alcoholic stupor starting to wear off. "Antje!" he muttered, then something about a shoe. Then clearly, "You ol' bastard!" It sounded like a bad dream, but whether good or bad, he no longer slept soundly, and somewhere within his waking consciousness, it registered the small, but unusual weight upon his chest. His eyelashes flickered; his eyes opened slightly, then instantly wide as one word shot through his brain: rat!

"Arrgh!" he bellowed, as he jerked forward. The poor kitten was flung into the air to land hard upon the brick floor. Kristoph fumbled for something to strike with. His hand knocked over the empty bottle then his fingers found the shoe. He slammed it down upon the kitten, but missed. The kitten had not even tried to move out of the way. It was all too much: the cold, the hunger, the hard brick, the bang of the shoe!

"Mew! Mew! Mew!" she cried.

Kristoph, poised to strike again, heard her cries; more than heard them, for they echoed something that had recently been very much on his own mind, and he knew exactly what those cries meant.

> *Why? Why? Why?*
> *Why is there so much pain?*
> *Why are you so cruel?*
> *Why is the world such a hard place?*

Kristoph dropped the shoe. Feeling sick, he leaned back in the chair and brought one hand to the lump on his forehead. Two incidents, which had occurred earlier that day, played over again in his mind, even against his wish to forget them.

The first had been an argument between himself and his younger brother, Matthys. Matthys, like all the men in the village, struggled to put sufficient food upon the table. Consequently, he had never been able to put away something for the future. That is why Matthys had approached Kristoph, seeking money for dowries for his three daughters, who were approaching marrying age. Kristoph had flatly refused this request, and Matthys, who rarely got angry, had cursed Kristoph and called him mean. Kristoph, in turn, called Matthys stupid and lazy and turned away in disgust.

Later, when Kristoph was walking home from his tavern, the door to his brother's house opened, and there had stood Antje, Matthys' wife. It had appeared to have been a coincidence, her opening the door just then, but Kristoph knew otherwise. Antje, carrying a heavy wash bowl in her sturdy arms, flung its contents of dirty water at his feet. This forced Kristoph to stop, annoyed that Antje had wet his boots.

"Matthys has gone to market in Dordrecht," Antje said.

"Whatever for?" Kristoph replied.

"To sell the cow," she said, adding, "for the girls' dowries."

Though hardened by years at sea, Kristoph was not a cruel man. Still, the idea of his brother thinking he could get anything for his rickety cow made him laugh.

Antje was not likewise amused. "Kristoph, you ol' bastard!" she screamed. She started to throw the bowl at him, but it was awkward for such use. Instead she took off her shoe and hurled it instead. Her aim was true and hit him square in the forehead. The surprise as much as the force of it knocked him off his feet, and he fell hard on the ice.

"Go to the devil!" Antje yelled, as Kristoph lay on his back.

In a rage, Kristoph struggled to rise, slipped and fell a second time. On hands his knees, he shook his fist, and called Antje every vile name he could summon from his rich seaman's vocabulary, not that it did much good as Antje had already slammed her door. He grabbed the shoe, intending to throw it through her window, then thought better. Shaking the shoe, he yelled, "See if you'll ever see this shoe again!" Kristoph stumbled away to his own house and quelled the fire of his anger in the oblivion of drink.

Why? Why? Why?

Had the kitten cried out once more, or had it been Kristoph's imagination? Either way, he did not know the answers to her questions.

"It is just the way of the world," he said. He looked down to see if the kitten was listening, but she had vanished. Surprised, he stood to light the lamp, but in moving, kicked the shoe and sent it skittering across the floor.

"Meeewwww!" cried the shoe in one long, piteous wail.

Kristoph retrieved the shoe and cradled it in his strong hands. Two small eyes, reflecting the moonlight, stared back at him. For the first time since his encounters with his Matthys and Antje, Kristoph smiled.

"Come out," he coaxed. "I'll not hurt you, I swear."

But the kitten had already suffered enough abuse for one night, and burrowed deep within the toe of the wooden shoe.

Kristoph set the shoe upon the kitchen table, and without bothering to light the lamp, for the moonlight was bright enough, he took from the cupboard a heavy ceramic jar. Lifting the lid, he extracted a piece of pickled herring and rinsed it in a bowl of water.

"Here you are, little one," he said, dangling a piece of fish in front of the kitten's face.

Smelling the fish, the kitten lashed out with a front paw.

Kristoph laughed as the tiny claws bit into his finger. "Not in there, little one. If you want this fish, you'll have to come out."

He did not have to repeat his demand. The kitten leapt out of the shoe and as fast as lightning, tore the fish from Kristoph fingers. In the time it took Kristoph to peel off another piece of fish, the first was gone.

"Mew!" cried the kitten, looking up at Kristoph.

"What?" Kristoph said, dangling the second piece in front of her. "You want more?"

The kitten made a leap for the fish, but this time Kristoph was faster.

"Mew!"

"All right, All right," Kristoph said, setting the fish upon the table, "I will not tease a hungry kitten."

As she ate, Kristoph rubbed the kitten's head with a calloused thumb. In response, a low growl issued from the kitten's throat.

"Now, now, there's no need to act like that. There's plenty more where that came from."

Kristoph turned the piece of fish over, for he had already stripped the first side clean, and separated the remaining flesh from the bones. "There," he said, dropping the fish on the table, "that's more meat than you've on your bones."

While the kitten ate, Kristoph carried the bowl to the door and threw the briny water out upon the snow. He thought he saw a light within his brother's house across the road, though perhaps it was a trick of the moonlight reflecting off the window. He wondered whether Matthys had returned from Dordrecht, and, if so, what, if anything, he had to show for his efforts?

Kristoph shut the door against the cold and moved to the fireplace where he stirred the embers and placed as few chunks of coal upon the grate. He returned to the table where the kitten sat washing her face. He picked her up and placed her on the mantelpiece next to the unlit oil lamp. The kitten didn't like being stranded on this high place and voiced her disapproval.

"Don't worry," Kristoph said, lifting the lampshade, "I'll not leave you there for long."

But the kitten would not wait, and leapt from the mantel onto Kristoph's beard then clambered onto his shoulder.

"My, aren't we impatient!" Kristoph remarked.

He struck a match to the lamp then pulled the chair closer to the fire and sat down. "Now let's see how many fleas you have." He found three fleas and flicked them into the fire. The kitten, in response to this grooming, purred contently then curled up on his lap. Kristoph stroked the kitten's head even after her little motor works ceased to putter and she settled silently into sleep. There was much on his mind, and most of it concerned the kitten's questions.

Why is there so much pain?

Pain and pleasure go hand in hand, he reasoned. That's just the way of it. He thought of the kitten: one moment cold and starving, the next warm and sated.

Why are you so cruel?

He was not cruel, at least not by his reckoning. At least, no crueler than the next man, and he knew men well, particularly those of his village.

Why was the world such a hard place?

Like pain, it was just the way things were. He had never known it otherwise. Yet would his life have been made easier if he had chosen differently, perhaps taken a wife and raised children as Matthys had done?

"You make your choices and you live with them." Odd this talking aloud, he thought. It had to be the presence of the kitten.

He leaned back in the chair, closed his eyes, but his mind was far too busy for sleep. He thought of his brother's request for money. As a mental exercise, he pondered the amount sufficient for a girl's dowry.

A gulden.

This response coming from some recess in his brain was like another blow to the head. A gulden! A man might work for a whole year and consider himself lucky to have a gulden to show for his efforts. He doubted he even possessed any.

Slowly, so as not to disturb the kitten, he stood and gently laid her upon his bed opposite the fireplace. Then he went to the window and drew the curtains, though it was very unlikely anyone would have looked in at that time of night. Beneath his bed there was a brick like all the others, only this one loose. Kneeling, he pried up the brick and removed a large bag from the hole beneath. He loosened the drawstring and poured the contents upon the bed. It made a sizable pile and atop this glittering mound of silver lay three guldens. The sight of them angered him, for it was as if the guldens were testing him. Three golden guldens, three daughters' dowries. He shook his head. How could he be thinking what he was thinking?

He hefted one of the coins. It was heavy, as it should be, for it represented countless nights in frigid weather when lesser men had already quit the sea. It represented distant and dangerous voyages when others were content with meager catches inshore. It represented daring raids upon the territories of rival fishing villages when need, or plain greed, had demanded it. How could he think of giving away what he had come by so hard?

For a long time, he remained kneeling beside the bed, studying the gleaming mound of coins. It wasn't the sacrifice of his hard work that troubled him as much as the fear that one day he might need the coins and not have them. Then again …

"All right, I'll do it!" He stood up and holding the three guldens, walked to the table and placed them in Antje's wooden shoe. "But they had better not ask for another copper! Not ever!"

Before he changed his mind, he took the shoe and went to the door and opened it. The moonlight was bright upon the snow. He shielded his eyes with one hand as he looked about. Of course, being the dead of night there was no one about, but under the circumstances, he had to be sure. Satisfied, he crept toward his brother's house. When he reached the door, he again looked around before placing Antje's shoe before the threshold then mounded the snow in front of it so the shoe could only be seen by a person opening the door. Then he stole back to his own house and quietly closed the door. His heart was pounding, his head throbbing. What had he done? He had always thought Matthys the stupider of the two brothers. Now, he knew better.

Feeling old and tired, he lifted the kitten so he could lay down. The kitten did not wake. It was a long time before Kristoph could join her in sleep.

"Kristoph! Kristoph!" cried Antje, pounding on Kristoph's door.

Kristoph, awakened from a troubled sleep, quietly moaned then rolled on to his side. He wanted her to go away.

Antje rattled the door, but it was bolted against her. She pounded on the door again. "Kristoph, I know you're in there!"

Kristoph was now fully awake. The light in the room was dim. He was glad he had closed the curtains; Antje would not be able to look in.

"Kristoph?" She sounded less certain now. Was he at home or not? There came a lighter rapping. "Kristoph?" More silence, then, "You ol' bastard."

How different her tone from the last time she had called him that! How tender her voice–and something else; Kristoph heard her joy.

It was not a feeling he shared. He lay, watching the kitten at play on the floor. She had found a button and thought this a great toy. She would bat it along the floor, then run after it, take it in her mouth, immediately drop it, then stare at it as if it were a thing alive and might run away, encourage it along with a soft pat, then bat it across the floor and repeat the game anew.

Kristoph considered getting up and building up the fire, but the smoke would announce his presence. Instead, he closed his eyes and fell asleep again.

It was not pounding that woke him later, but his need to urinate. Throwing back his covers, he pulled the chamber pot from beneath the bed, set it on a chair and used it while standing. When finished, he buttoned his trousers, then scratched his scalp with both hands. Now that he was up, he must decide what to do. If he went to the tavern, Antje would discover him and certainly plague him with her gratitude. This troubled him less than knowing the furor that would erupt once others learned of what he had done. He realized he must get away from the village! Away without anyone seeing him!

A movement attracted his attention. The kitten had managed to climb onto the table and was sniffing the edges of water left from the night before. He snatched her by the nape of her neck then with his free hand, swept the water onto the floor. Dropping the kitten hard upon the table, he lifted the lid of the jar with the herring.

"Everyone wants something from me!" he grumbled.

This time he didn't bother to rinse the fish, but tore off a large section of flesh and tossed it onto the table. The kitten appeared not to mind the saltiness, and as she ate, Kristoph cautiously lifted a corner of the window curtain and peered out. Happily, there was a fog so thick he could not see his brother's house just across the road.

He let the curtain fall, then scratched his cheek, thinking. The fog would mask his escape, but where could he go? Then it occurred to him that if Matthys could go to Dordrecht, so could he. He would be getting a late start, but that was all the better, for he was not planning to return until everyone in the village was asleep. He might even stay the night in Dordrecht.

Now that he had a plan, he moved quickly. He pulled on his heavy boots, then took a wool sweater from his sea chest followed by his black wool coat. Then a soft cap, and a scarf around his neck. He never owned a pair of gloves, for gloves were an encumbrance when at sea, but he had his deep coat pockets to keep his hands warm.

Having completed his dress, he patted his trouser pockets to check that he had sufficient coin, then put his pipe and tobacco into a coat pocket. Finally, he looked around the room to see if there was anything he had forgotten.

The kitten, having finished her breakfast, was peering over the edge of the table, trying to figure a way down. Kristoph dropped her into his other coat pocket as if she were no more than a ring of keys.

"Mew!" the kitten cried.

"Hush!" Kristoph warned her. He did want her cries announcing his departure. He opened the door a few inches and looked out. The fog was now so thick even the road disappeared within a few feet. He stood listening, but the only sound was the intermittent clang of a ship's bell. He closed the door and strode quickly away. The crunch of his boots upon the snow sounded like the discharge of cannons to his ears, but no one challenged him. After a few minutes walking, he relaxed. He reached for his pipe and tobacco, but into the wrong pocket. The kitten pounced upon his fingers. Laughing, he pulled her out.

"Are you ready for a bit of adventure, little one?" he said, holding her before his face.

"Mew," she answered.

He raised the collar of his coat and tucked the kitten between it and the back of his neck. The kitten, pleased with her lofty perch, purred and kneaded Kristoph's scarf.

Kristoph found his pipe, packed it with tobacco, lit it, and drew in the sweet smoke. He exhaled with a sigh of satisfaction. His pipe warmed him; the kitten's purring pleased him; the trampled roadway was easy to follow; and he was glad to have gotten away so easily. Feeling very content, he let his legs gather in the pleasant miles, and by the time he reached Dordrecht, it was early afternoon and the fog had lifted.

Upon entering the town, Kristoph discovered there was a fair in progress. He did not immediately plunge into the festivities, which were in full swing, but hung back, observing. Vendors were busy selling food from booths. Craftsmen hawked their wares from the backs of wagons. But more than commerce was happening. High above the heads of a spell-bound audience, an acrobat balanced upon a rope. Not to be outdone, two jugglers tossed belaying pins between them, while each keeping three more suspended in the air. There was a man who inhaled swords and another who exhaled fire. Music from different groups of musicians reached his ears, mixed together in a merry cacophony. How this pageantry mocked the solemn poverty of his own village!

Yet this joyous spectacle did not add to Kristoph's contentment, for he was a quiet man, an inward man, always awkward in crowds. True, he owned a tavern, but that had come to him by chance, not choosing, and he left the running of it to others while he hid in the storage room and smoked and drank and occasionally played chess with a few old cronies.

Now, as he watched the frolickers, he felt uneasy. He stood in the road not knowing what to do. Having walked so far, it seemed foolish to just turn around and go back home. Besides, if he did, he would return to find his village still awake.

Absorbed in his thoughts, Kristoph had forgotten the kitten until he saw her in the roadway ahead of him marching forward with upturned tail. It seemed *she* felt no reluctance to join the merrymaking. Smiling, Kristoph hurried forward, scooped the kitten up, and placed her upon his shoulder.

"Very well. We'll go have a bit of supper and some ale. But then we're going home!"

But if Kristoph thought to pass through the crowds unnoticed, he was much mistaken, for he could hardly take a step without someone remarking upon the beautiful, snow-white kitten and asking Kristoph for permission to hold her. For the kitten, this was heaven, for in addition to much fondling and adoration, she received many delicacies of food, which forced Kristoph to wonder whether mere fish would ever again suffice.

As for Kristoph, he was drawn into conversations he never would have struck up on his own, and, to his surprise, he found these idle chats pleasurable. And once he started to enjoy himself, he started to purchase things, and once he started to purchase things, he could not seem to stop. It did not trouble him that he bought the fish pies, or the tankard of ale, for these were welcomed after a long walk and would provide sustenance for the journey home. And a bit of toffee was all right, for he liked to indulge his sweet tooth now and then.

But what of the other things? Did he truly need a new pipe and more tobacco? A new cap? New scarf? Wool socks, perhaps, but two pair? And gloves of all things! And why did he think the kitten needed a fine piece of woven cloth for a new bed?

With feelings bounding between exaltation and horror, Kristoph passed over his money and received small treasures in return. He was even forced to purchase a basket to carry it all. He knew he had gone around the bend when he bought a bar of lavender-scented soap!

It was a relief when he discovered he had circled through the streets and back to where he started, for now he had seen everything there was to purchase. He found an empty bench away from the crowd and sat down to rest his tired legs and examine his purchases. Leaning forward he looked with bewilderment into the basket set on the ground at his feet. The kitten, atop his shoulder, looked down also.

"It must have been something they put in the ale," he explained to her. "Makes a man a fool."

What was happening to him? This buying madness on the heels of yesterday's munificence? Yet when he thought about the guldens he had given his nieces, he realized he had given nothing to Matthys and Antje.

Quickly, he rummaged through the contents of the basket. The pipe and tobacco he would give to Matthys, as well as a pair of socks. Also, the gloves. For Antje, there was the bar of soap and the basket itself, which were women's things anyway.

He sat back and idly ran his fingers through the tangle of his beard. He wanted to give Antje something else, something special. He looked to the west, where the setting sun was a watery smear in the overcast sky. With the coming darkness, merchants and craftsmen were starting to close their booths and pack their wagons. Kristoph stood, swept up his basket, then strode back into the fair, for he wanted to make one last purchase.

He wandered about in growing frustration until he finally found the wagon he remembered. The merchant, a sad-looking cobbler, was packing away his tools and unsold shoes with the help of his tired wife, while their two small children slept upon a bed of straw in their wagon. The cobbler was happy to unpack crates so that Kristoph could make a purchase. The cobbler's wife helped Kristoph select a pair of shoes to fit Antje – leather shoes, not wooden. Once he paid for the shoes, Kristoph had but two copper pennies left. He hesitated before placing these into the hand of the surprised woman.

"For the children," he explained.

Then he lifted his basket, now heavier by the addition of the shoes, and made toward the road that would take him home. Outside the ebbing crowd, he stopped to button his coat, for with the setting of the sun, the temperature had begun to fall. The poor kitten sat upon his shoulder shivering. Kristoph lifted her off his shoulder and tucked her inside his warm coat pocket. Then he hoisted his basket, and moved briskly down the road, for he had a long way to go, and already he yearned for bed.

It was well after midnight when he saw his little house and the moonlight reflecting off it. He knew it would be a cold house that greeted him, but he was too tired to care. He pushed open the door and, to his surprise, was met with a gush of warm air. The oil lamp, resting on the table, provided a welcome light. Dropping his basket beside the lamp, he looked around and saw things had been altered. The floor had been scrubbed. The fireplace, which held a good fire, had been cleared of its accumulation of ash. The chamber pot, which he had left on the chair, had been returned to its rightful place under the bed, and the bed made up. As for the bed, gone was the bed cover fashioned from an old sheet of sail cloth, and in its place, a quilt. It was not a new one, yet little worn, and with an applique of pretty red flowers and green vines only just starting to fade.

Kristoph fingered the quilt. "Women's stuff," he muttered, but was pleased, nonetheless. He folded back the covers which released the fresh smell of laundry soap. Carefully, he removed the kitten from his pocket and set her upon the fresh bedding where she stretched out until she was twice her length before curling up to go to sleep.

Kristoph then threw off his coat and, rubbing his hands together, approached the table, for on it sat a pitcher of ale, and under a piece of cloth, a loaf of baked bread still a little warm. Not bothering with a knife, he tore off a chunk of bread and stuffed it into his mouth. This he washed down with ale drunk straight from the pitcher. Wiping his mouth with the end of his beard, he looked about the room and liked what he saw. His mantel, which had not been dusted in memory, was gleaming from an application of furniture oil. The chair fabric had been brushed, and a tear on the seat cushion sewn. Had he been more observant, he would have also noticed a small hole in his wall had been plugged with oakum.

These many kindnesses made Kristoph happy, happier than when he won his tavern in the card game. And he knew who to thank. He was out his door and nearly to his brother's house before he remembered it was the middle of the night and Antje, along with everyone else, would be asleep. Still, he was tempted to pound upon his brother's door and rouse them all out of bed, for he felt an impishness that was the product of his elation. Resisting this temptation, he turned to go home, but in turning, he happened to glance at the house next to his brother's and saw something lying outside its door. Curious, he went to investigate. What he discovered made his happiness vanish, and his head to throb under the pressure of a quickening pulse, for in front of the door, side-by-side, were two wooden shoes.

He hurried to the next house where it was just as he feared, more wooden shoes, this time five. Alarmed, he ran down the road and at every house it was the same: wooden shoes in front of each door, only the number varied. Swearing under his breath, he clenched his fists. He should have known that word of his generosity would make him the target of opportunists. Well, he knew just the way to put an end to this mischief! He would gather up all the shoes and burn them, and tomorrow when the villagers were walking about in their stocking feet, he would savor a warm fire fueled at their expense! What a laugh that would be!

Yet when he started to instigate this excellent plan, he of a sudden saw matters with a clarity that had nothing to do with the brightness of the moon. As he slowly walked along the row of houses, he saw not only the crumbling walls, but the people who dwelled within them. Here lived a widow struggling to feed her two children; here was a child with a club foot; here a father addicted to drink; here the parents of two children dead from scarlet fever; next door, a young father on whose eyes cataracts were growing; and across the street another young man whose father had thrown away his son's inheritance in a game of cards. He realized that every house had been visited by some tragedy, save one, the house which he now stood in front of: his own. Why did it appear shabbier than all the others, for was he not by far the richest man in the village? He opened his door and again was greeted with brightness and warmth, only this time they gave him no cheer. He shut

The Dreams of Gerontius

the door and leaned against it. Once again he felt the madness coming upon him and knew he would be helpless to fight it. This time he did not bother with the curtains, but went straight to the hideaway and extracted the bag of money. Next he took down from the mantelpiece, a dusty Bible, which served as a repository for important papers, and from this, he removed an envelope. Then he put on his coat, for he could not stop trembling.

As Kristoph made his way back along the row of houses, he placed money into every shoe. Though generous, he did not place an equal amount into each, but where the need was greater, he put more. And into one particular shoe, he placed the envelope containing the cherished deed to his tavern.

When Kristoph at last returned home, he tossed the moneybag, and it hit upon the table with hardly a sound. He did not trouble to remove his coat, but sat upon his bed feeling drained of life. The kitten, awake, tried to climb upon his lap, but he pushed her away. Yet when she approached a second time, he received her and gently scratched her head. Then with a shudder, he leaned forward and to the stain of his beard, he added the salt of his tears. He despised himself for his weakness, yet what was that compared to this feeling in his chest, for a crack had opened in his heart which could not be plugged with oakum, and he cried with the pain of it, and for all he would lose by it. In his mind he saw his remaining years as a constant surrendering until all he had accumulated by strength was lost by his own weakness and stupidity. Then what would become of him?

· Gerontius ·

I'd forgotten just how sad and beautiful your dream was, Serena. I was moved to tears to hear you tell of that poor kitten's struggle to get through the wall, in part because a kitten has been hiding out under the tool shed in the community garden, and I had promised myself I would look after her and see that she got enough to eat. But then Michael had his important concert, and there was the big brouhaha with Marshall Banks, and before that the rooftop lecture series, of which I was the event coordinator, and with all that and everything else, I'm afraid I haven't been as good as my word.

The fact is, I'm to blame for the kitten's plight, though the irony of it is that I was just trying to do a good deed. For weeks, I plotted to free Yum-Yum from the prison of his stamp-sized yard, figuring not only would he be less neurotic if he had the run of the neighborhood, but it would give him something more to talk about than the joys of chasing after moldy tennis balls. Unfortunately, asphalt had been laid right up to the fence, making it impossible to dig a way out. But clever me found a weak spot where weeds had broken up the pavement. Of course, a cat's claws are wasted on digging, which is better left to dogs, for they are forever digging holes to hide away some tidbit for future consumption. (I ask you, who but a dog would want to eat something that's been buried a week?) Naturally, I left the grunt work to Yum-Yum while I supervised. The hardest part was getting him to understand this was not some game, but an actual jail break. But after only an hour or two of explaining, I got him digging in the right spot. I, myself, levered out the last chunk of asphalt that separated Yum-

Yum from freedom.

And what was the first thing Yum-Yum did to celebrate his liberation? His piddled on half the tires in the parking lot. I had thought to be his guide to this brave new world, but was so disgusted with him, I decided to let him go his own way, convinced that his next priority would be hunting up turds.

But it was a mistake to let Yum-Yum go off unattended, for as I was making my way back up the fire escape to our apartment, I heard the cries of a cat in distress. I streaked across the parking lot and into the community garden where I found a young tabby fighting for her life with that insufferable Yum-Yum. I immediately joined the battle, leaping upon Yum-Yum and sinking my teeth into his ear. He yelped and darted crossways through rows of corn with me riding his back. I was so mad, I wanted to scratch his eyes out. So, this is how you repay me for my kindness!

Then I realized he was just a dog, a dumb brute, nature's lowliest creature. So, I let Yum-Yum go then raced back to find the tabby lying upon her side, alive, but only just. I did what I could. I bathed her wounds, which were horrible to behold. I sat by her head and tried to comfort her with my purring, to which she responded with a weak little purr of her own. And when the breath of life left her body, I closed her eyes and said a benediction, one that I think struck the right balance between sentiment and practicality:

> *May your every earthly trial be a nice fat gopher in your new life to come.*

But the tabby's death was not the worst of it, for now I saw what I failed to see before: the bodies of four kittens scattered along a row of cabbages. Evidently, Yum-Yum had shaken the poor things until he had broken their necks. I carried each one to where their mother lay and arranged them in repose beside her. Needless to say, I went from the garden low in spirit. I returned a few days later to find that some kind soul had buried them, marking the graves with one standing stone ringed with four smaller ones. Blinking back tears, I sat down to pay my respects and to reflect upon life's transitory nature.

Then I saw a gopher out of the corner of my eye, and since it is a general policy with me never to let lofty thoughts take precedent over a snack, I leaped after it. Alas, he quickly burrowed in under the tool shed, a place so low to the ground, I lost my chance to enlighten him on the subject of life's impermanency. Still, I stuck my head in as far under as I could, only to have my nose scratched by tiny claws. As I sat back, rubbing my poor proboscis, I realized the scratch was not the work of a gopher, whose duller claws I was well acquainted with. It seemed one of the kittens had escaped being Yum-Yummed.

I tried to coax the poor thing out, but she was still too traumatized to trust that my intentions were good. The best thing I could do under the circumstances was to provide her with the comfort of a meal. At the time, there was a family of mice living amongst the zucchini. I chose the fattest one, brought it back, still alive, to the shed where I kept a paw on its tail to keep it from running away. When the squirming mouse elicited no response from the kitten, I let it run about a little, just to assure the kitten it was the real thing. This prompted a glimpse of a white whisker, but nothing more.

So, I resorted to a stronger enticement: I bit the mouse's head off and shoved the rest in under the shed with just the tail sticking out. For myself, nothing arouses the appetite like the sound of someone gnawing away upon some delicacy. It was the same with the kitten, for as I crunched upon the mouse head, the tail of the mouse slowly disappeared. Licking my lips, I vowed I would lure the kitten from her hideaway even if it meant depleting my entire supply of mice.

But as the poet said, "way leads on to way," and the paths of the next couple of weeks took me in directions much traveled.

But now, Serena, I'm determined, just as soon as you and Michael decide to call it a night, to go see if the kitten is still out there hiding under the shed.

But first, I must hear the rest of your dream.

The Three Dowries (concluded)

A wake! Awake!

Kristoph, who just a little while earlier had fallen asleep sitting up, worked to open his eyes.

Awake! cries the watchman, high in his tower.

"I am awake," Kristoph muttered. Or was he dreaming, for surely he was hearing the voices of angels?

Arise, take up your lantern!

Kristoph stumbled to his door, and upon opening it, was immediately assaulted with a blast of frigid air, for the fog had returned.

Glory be sung to you with tongues of men and angels!

Kristoph was right! The voices were those of angels, angels gathered in a half circle about his house. Still half asleep, he rubbed his eyes. No, they were not angels, though the people of his village looked like angels, for each carried a lighted candle whose light was reflected in the fog, ringing each singer in halo of gold.

The villagers sang with voices sweet and clear.

With harps and beautiful cymbals, we are consorts of the

angels, high around Your Throne.

Kristoph felt a small presence rubbing against a stockinged foot. He picked up the kitten and placed her upon his shoulder as the villagers continued to sing.

No eye has ever seen, no ear has ever heard such joy.

Kristoph could see the joy in the faces of the singers. Moreover, he felt some of that joy in his own breast wherein, not so long ago, there lodged only pain.

Lo! Lo! We sing in sweet rejoicing.

The chorale came to an end, and there was an awkward silence as the villagers waited in uneasy anticipation of Kristoph's response. As Kristoph surveyed his neighbors, he saw smiling faces dissolve into looks of uncertainty. Little children looked like frightened rabbits. Is that how they see me, Kristoph wondered, as a man to be feared? Or maybe they think me mad to have given away my money and fear that, any second, I will demand its return.

Kristoph was not a man of words. What could he say to convince his neighbors that he was not that man he saw in their eyes?

The kitten nudged Kristoph's chin with her head. A little girl giggled at the sight, only to be hushed by her mother.

Cradling the kitten in his rough hands, Kristoph held her out before him, as if she were an offering. "This little kitten somehow made it into my house." He smiled. "I think she also made it into my heart."

Hearing this, smiles returned.

"I …" Kristoph did not know what else to say, other than, "You all sing like angels!"

The villagers laughed then began to sing once more:

Blessed are those who, through compassion, bear the weight of others' suffering,
Who, with pity for the wretched, pray steadfastly for them.
They who are helpful in word, and, if possible, in deed,
Shall in turn receive His help, and they themselves receive compassion.

Kristoph was not a man of faith. He had given little thought to the existence of a God, benevolent or otherwise. Furthermore, he had never asked for help from anyone. Now as he listened to words being sung, he felt his old self dissipating, as if it were a fog being burned off by the sun.

What did this mean?

Seeking answers in the faces of his neighbors, he felt the divide between them and himself likewise dissipating, and, perhaps for the first time in his life, he felt himself not singular, but a part of a greater whole. A madness had driven him to give away his wealth, and he expected to suffer thereby. But had it been madness, or was it need, for where was the dividing line between giving and receiving?

As Kristoph stood, listening, a feeling of hope was kindled in his heart; hope not for a future characterized by loss, but one to be greeted with bright anticipation of gifts to be given and gifts to be received, as now, this day, with a sharp joy, the voices of his neighbors, his friends, sang in his heart.

· Serena ·

"I think that toward the end of my dream, I was half-awake. The villagers in my dream were singing to Kristoph, but at the same time I was hearing a boys' choir on the radio."

"Singing a Bach chorale by the sound of it," Michael said.

"Yes. It was actually a lovely way to be woken." Serena stroked Gerontius' head. "Gerry-cat brought me a very sweet dream."

"Well, I prefer yours to mine. Yours was like *The Christmas Carol*, only instead of Scrooge's redemption being driven by the ghosts of Christmases past, present and future, you had the poor little kitten who'd lost her mitten. But if you're into interpreting dreams, I can't see how this one relates to you. You're certainly not a greedy miser like Scrooge or Kristoph."

"Actually, the dream is very much about me."

Michael looked around the room. "What? You got a cache of money stashed away somewhere?"

"Don't I wish. But I wasn't thinking about the money. To me, this dream was about belonging." Serena looked out the window. "That night I saw Gerontius out there on the fire escape, looking all cold and miserable, was a night that I was feeling very lonely, and I'd have to say rather fragile."

"I'm sorry."

"Don't be. I'm used to it. At least the lonely part. I don't make friends easily. I guess I'm not what you would call a people person."

Michael rubbed his foot against hers. "You seem friendly enough to me."

Serena pulled her foot away. "Don't toy with me, Michael!"

"I'm not, Serena. I wouldn't do that, not with you. I truly enjoy your company. I enjoy talking about these silly dreams we've been having."

Serena returned her foot to rest against Michael's leg. "I actually do better with people when it's just one-to-one. I don't think I could do what you do, work with a troupe of performers, a lot of whom you probably don't even know."

"Yeah, but that's different. It's not like we're just standing around, drinking and bullshitting. We're there for a specific purpose, to work on a piece of music, and when the performance is over, I never see a lot of those people again."

"Yet I imagine it must be nice to be part of something, to be part of a community."

Michael pointed to Serena's loom. "Isn't there a community of weavers?"

"I know a few weavers. But weaving is a rather solitary art. For one thing, it's not like I can drag a loom over to someone else's house."

"May I ask if you that's how you make a living?"

"Weaving?" Serena laughed. "If you total up all the work that goes into a weaving project and compare that with what I can sell it for, I'm probably not even making minimum wage."

"So how do you pay the bills?"

"I work in a cytology lab, which is another solitary endeavor; it's just me, my microscope, and a bunch of slides. It's not my idea of an ideal job, but it pays the bills and allows me to spend my free time doing something I truly enjoy: working with fibers."

"I hope you don't mind me saying, but it seems you choose to be lonely."

"I know. So, it's rather silly of me to complain. But I don't think it's just me; there are other factors."

"Such as?"

"Well, I know this is going to sound a bit strange, but I often feel like I don't belong here. Do you ever feel like you were born in the wrong century?"

"Not really. I don't yearn for outhouses. And let me say for the record, because I think it fits in with this, part of me goes out to Kristoph, the old Kristoph, before he found redemption at the paws of a kitten. I think he had a right to feel rotten about giving away his money. This idea of wealth being somehow bad is an antiquated notion. Hell, who doesn't want to be rich? And it wasn't like Kristoph robbed a bank. He worked hard for his money."

"So, you're saying that Kristoph was wrong to share his money?"

"I'm not saying he was right or wrong."

"But you called him a greedy miser."

"I got caught up in the pathos of the story. It makes you feel all warm and fuzzy inside. Here's this old curmudgeon who becomes this really good guy. But in my experience, stories like these really don't make a lasting impression. You read them, you sigh, maybe brush a tear away, then ten minutes later you're back doing whatever it is you feel like doing, and nothing has changed."

"And you're saying that's good?"

"I'm saying that's the way it is. We all think of ourselves first, and I don't think that's necessarily a bad thing. I want to be a great singer. Is that wrong? I want to be famous. I want to sing in Carnegie Hall, and I would have if Gerontius hadn't screwed it up for–Ouch!"

"Gerontius!" Serena scolded "That wasn't very nice."

Michael sucked on the back of his hand where Gerontius had sunk his claws.

"Do you need a Band-Aid, Michael?"

"I think so. He got me pretty good."

Serena got up off the window seat. "Let me take you to the bathroom where we can wash your hand and put some antiseptic on it."

Holding his wounded hand, Michael followed Serena. "See? I told you Gerontius was a schizo devil."

· Gerontius ·

"Schizo devil!" Now I almost wish I had bitten you as well. Still, it was wrong of me to scratch you, Michael. It is just that I've had it up to my whiskers with your blaming me for ruining your chance to sing in Carnegie Hall. If anyone's responsible, it is you, for refusing to sing the part of Gerontius in that high, simpering little voice Banks was pushing on you. Working on your upper register, indeed! Banks had you squealing away like Miss Piggy with a quarter wedged up her nose.

Excuse me, there I go trying to sound clever again. Another reason I dislike wit is that it is often cruel, something I have no wish to be, so let me take another tack.

What you perceive to be a failure, Michael—being passed over by Marshall Banks—I see as evidence of an inner strength that you seldom reveal. I am not even sure you're aware of it, yet when it pops up, it shows that you possess the spirit of a true artist.

What strength am I talking about? To fully explain, I must do like Serena and "set the scene a little," which first requires me to say a little something about Edward Elgar's magnificent oratorio, *The Dream of Gerontius.*

As you know, it is a setting of a poem by Cardinal John Newman. I actually met Newman once, long before he was a cardinal, before he had even joined the Catholic church. Our paths crossed in Oxford where I was sharing a house with a professor of ornithology, a field of study I thought completely unworthy of him. I remember it was a sunny April day, with just a touch of wind, and I was venturing out to do a bit of hunting on Glouchester Green when I spotted a man, his nose in a book, inching along George Street. When a particular absorbing passage brought him to a stop, I took the opportunity to rub up against his legs, for his shins had pronounced ridges, made perfect for scratching my back.

John Newman looked down upon me, smiled, then snapped his book shut and bent down to scratch between my ears. At that moment, I felt his full attention upon me. What is more, I sensed that I was to him not just a cat, but a unique soul, a divine being, the sparrow whose falling does not go unnoticed. Need I tell you how this made me feel, how I purred so hard I nearly broke my purr-box? And then he blessed me with this:

> *How should ethereal natures comprehend a thing*
> *made up of spirit and of clay,*
> *Were we not tasked to nurse it and to tend,*
> *linked one to one throughout its mortal day?*

Cardinal Newman was to use these same lines in his great poem to describe how angels wait upon men. Yet on that fair April day, I felt he was referring to the two of us, for, in our own ways, we both had been called upon to serve mankind.

Late in his life, Cardinal Newman was moved to write *The Dream of Gerontius* following a serious illness. It is the story of a man's death and his ascension to the throne of God, and Elgar's setting of it combines a reverence for the text with the sensitivity of an artist at the height of his creative power.

The role of Gerontius requires a wide range of vocal color. At times, the singer must express fear, for Gerontius is, after all, embarking on that voyage into the great unknown. Yet he must also reveal the strength that comes from faith, for it is faith that lifts Gerontius above his fear. But mostly the singer must express wonder, for Gerontius, free of mortal flesh, is ushered by angels into the very presence of God!

Obviously, the role of Gerontius is one that must be approached with due reverence. Yet Banks had you quavering like the Cowardly Lion with the Tin Man bouncing on his tail. And you went along with him, Michael, whining away in that little head voice of yours until hearing the two of you rehearse made me want to bite you both. (No, Michael, that was not the reason I bit Banks; I shall get to that.)

Yet when the moment of truth came, when you stood on stage before all those people, something moved you to forgo the simpering affectations and sing with all the feeling and power you possess. I am certain Banks was furious, and that is no doubt the real reason he refused to acknowledge you during the audience's applause, and why he is not taking you with him to Carnegie Hall. Still, you made the wise choice; it was the true artist in you, rising to the fore. To hear you sing was to be there with Gerontius in the presence of God and the heavenly host. It was one of the few times in my many lives, Michael, when I felt what only can be described as "awe." I do not know whether you will ever be a great singer, but I do know you sang like one tonight.

Now let me tell you a thing or two you don't know about your beloved Marshall Banks. Besides being a great choral conductor and a world class egotist, he is also a kleptomaniac. I did not make a fuss when he took some valuable scores from out of your piano bench, and I am sure you would have gladly given him your autographed copy of *Great Singers on Great Singing* had he asked, which he did not. But then his thieving eye fell upon something I knew you truly treasured, a small figure of a cat carved out of blood-red carnelian. I have often seen you hold it in your palm as you admired the minute details rendered by a gifted carver. And I have noticed your ritual of placing it next to your sheet music each time you begin to learn a new piece. The cat is obviously a talisman, something of magical power, and there was Banks, practically salivating over it as you were away using the bathroom.

Well, what was I to do? I snatched up the figurine an instant before Banks' sticky fingers latched onto it. Was Maestro Banks happy? He swept me up and pinned me under one arm then proceeded to try to pry open my jaws using a ballpoint pen. A ball point pen! Oh, how I wanted to sink my teeth into his forearm. Yet had I opened my mouth he would have snatched the little cat and pocketed it. I had only one recourse: I swallowed the figurine then gave maestro Banks the benefit of my fangs.

Of course, right then you happened to emerge from the bathroom. I imagine to your eye it looked like Banks had been holding me in his arms, perhaps petting me, when I lit into him. Little wonder then that you took Banks' side and was all sympathy for him and failed to take notice of my poor bleeding gums.

Then later when you returned from taking Banks to the doctor, you came at me once again with a broom, forcing me to spend another uncomfortable night on the fire escape, which made me wonder why I had gone to the trouble of saving your precious little figurine.

Speaking of the figurine, I thought it would have made an appearance by now, though how can I tell when you never clean out my litter box? I have done my best to shovel out the old turds (dropping them on that loathsome Yum-Yum) in my search, but even so, I may never find it, which would serve you right, Michael. My gums are still sore.

· Serena ·

"Well," Michael said, smoothing down the bandage on his hand as he reclaimed his place on the window seat, "I think this is proof that Gerontius is feeling better."

"I wonder if he needs to go out." Serena leaned over and opened the window. "It's getting stuffy in here, anyway."

"It must be all my hot air," Michael said.

"Why Michael, was that a bit of self-deprecating humor?"

"It must be your influence, teaching me to be humbler. But what were we talking about before Gerontius so rudely interrupted?"

"You were saying that people tend to think of themselves first, which is not necessarily a bad thing."

"Right."

"But that's precisely the reason why I feel I don't belong here. We live in a day when individual freedom is prized above all things, at least in this country. The idea of community, of a person's primary interests being in other people, is almost reviled."

"But you said you're not a people person."

"I know I said that, but I think what I really meant was that I'm not a people person with *that* type of person."

"The independent type, someone like me."

"Michael, I'm thinking out loud, here, so bear with me. I'm saying I find it difficult to feel close to people when all they care about is seeing how much they can get for themselves. We've elevated ego-gratification to a Constitutional right. And to someone like me, who's not all that interested in acquiring things, or making a lot of money, or getting power, or having it over other people, it's all …"

"A bit overwhelming?"

"It's downright scary. I feel like I'm a sheep in a land of jackals. Where are my people, Michael? Where are the people who value goodness above getting-ness?"

"They're all in novels by Jane Austen. They're all good and proper and civil, and they're all works of fiction because in the real world, people are a lot more complex than that. I also think you must not get out enough, because I know there are plenty of good people out there. You just have to get out and find them."

"I *do* get out, Michael. I drive to work and invariably some jerk rides my bumper because I'm only doing the speed limit. If I try to blot him out by listening to the radio, I get some call-in show with the host extolling the virtues of hurting people, or a guy rapping to what sounds like a jack hammer about the glories of violence and drugs, or at the very least, some pimply punk whining cause his girl ain't putting out for him. And all of this is really just the subtext. The real message is to buy; buy whatever the radio advertiser is pushing because that's what'll make you happy.

"And then when I get to work, John, my lab partner, who's not there half the time, is always pushing me to try one of his little pills, 'to make the day go better.' Yes, Michael, I *do* get out, and that's why I prefer to come home, lock my door, and weave."

Michael grinned.

"God, I hate it when you smile at me like that!"

"I'm sorry, Serena, I can't help it. It's just that, listening to you, I get the feeling that you're wound a little tight."

"Thank you, I should be nonchalant about bullies trying to run me down, or talking heads spewing hatred, or my lab partner trying to turn me into a dope fiend."

Michael shook his head. "That's not what I mean. Those things are awful, but not all the world is like that."

"But that's my point, Michael, the world *is* like that, at least it is to me, and it's only getting worse."

"Well, I don't see it that way, but that said, how would you make things different? You'd have us live like Kristoph, in little villages where everyone's poor but at least they love each other and go out of their way to convert wayward sinners by singing Bach chorales?"

"Don't scoff at love; it's the only thing truly worth having. It's what we are meant for: to love and be loved in return. You ask me what I'd like? I'd like to live in a more human world, without all the machines, the electronic do-dads, the mindless stuff. I'd like the pleasures of life to be human pleasures: talking to friends and neighbors. I'd like to live in a community of loving, caring people so I'd never have to be afraid to walk down my own street. I'd like to open my windows and instead of hearing the roar of cars and the blare of televisions, hear the voices of people calling out to each other. I want to hear voices, Michael. I want to hear talking and laughter and singing, and yes even yelling and crying if it comes from an actual human and not out of a television set. I want a world where people take joy in other people. I want—"

"To dance?"

"What?"

"Dance. You know, where people move together in time to music. Dance, one of the most intimate ways people communicate with one another."

"I know what dance is, Michael."

"Well, would you like to?"

"You mean, here? Now?"

Michael got up off the window seat and extended his hand to Serena.

"But Michael, it's the middle of the night."

"It's never too late to start living in a more human world."

"We'll wake the neighbors."

"No, we won't. We won't even play any music. I'll just hum a tune."

Serena bit her lower lip.

"Dance with me, Serena."

"But I don't know how."

"Neither do I."

Michael took Serena's hand and pulled her from the window seat, then as he hummed a waltz, they moved across the floor in stockinged feet.

· Gerontius ·

Seeing the two of you dancing together reminds me of Berlin back of my old caternity days. How you would have loved it, Serena, for it was the greatest time to be human, or feline for that matter, for so many of human pleasures are enjoyed by cats as well. Painting was a popular pastime, and every Sunday afternoon, when the weather was warm, dozens of artists could be seen in the parks, leaning over their canvases. Cats were a particularly popular subject, and I had the pleasure of sitting in the shade of a linden tree while an artist painted my portrait.

But most popular of all was dancing. Back then you could have danced any night of the week, no matter who you were or what your station in life. If not in the grand palaces, then in the music halls, or the taverns, or even in the streets.

And the music! When people danced, they danced to *real* music played by *real* people—orchestras, brass bands, polka bands, accordion bands, folk bands. When there was no band, people danced to a piano or any instrument they could find. The point is, people danced, they played music, they sang. Though the times were fraught with peril and physical hardships, they were rich in human fellowship.

Nowadays, you humans have everything turned on its head; you live a life of ease, yet there is so little joy in it. I could give you innumerable examples, but this one should suffice.

Earlier I mentioned the fire escape with its ladder to the roof. One of my jobs as event coordinator for the lecture series was to find a suitable venue, preferably a rooftop, which has always been a traditional meeting place for cats. The rooftop of our apartment building with its fine view of the city seemed ideal. The only drawback was access, for even a young cat finds a ladder daunting, and many of those attending the lectures were far from young, particularly the lecturers.

My problem was solved by Walter, a man I first knew by name only, for often as I sat out on the fire escape of an evening, I would hear his wife's complaining, even above the blare of the nightly news coming from the other apartments. It was, "Walter this," and "Walter that," and always in a tone of voice most people reserve for things found in a drain pipe, and always to make known her displeasure of Walter's habits, chief among them his smoking. In my caternity days, smoking was nearly as popular as dancing. In fact, it was practically an art form. Men prided themselves on the splendor of their pipes and judged their blends of tobacco as assiduously as wine connoisseurs judged blends of wine.

But for better or worse, times have changed, and Walter was forced to take his unwelcome habit to the rooftop where he could smoke in peace. And that is where we met. I happen to like the smell of tobacco smoke; I love to lick it off my fur. It is little wonder that Walter and I soon became fast friends. We would sit together of an evening and watch the lights of the city come on. Often he would enjoy a beer with his cigarette, and was kind enough to share some of it with me. And sensing my reluctance to use the ladder, he used a brick to wedge open the door that leads to the inner stairway, allowing me, and all those attending the lecture series, to come and go as we pleased.

I would like to think we paid Walter back, for he appeared to take interest in our lectures. He would bring a lawn chair and sit and smoke and give his undivided attention to the speaker. Due to the language barrier, I am not sure how much he got out of it. He certainly never spoke up during the Q&A. I think it was camaraderie he enjoyed, for it seemed to fill a great void in his life.

Yet I don't believe Walter's case was in anyway unusual, for I look out at night from the fire escape and see in every apartment, in nearly every room, a television going, very often watched by just one person. Then I look down to the streets and see how, save for automobiles whizzing their way to someplace else, they are deserted. Yet in those long-ago nights in Berlin, the streets would be filled with people out to enjoy the evening air. Now when someone ventures out, she does so with reluctance, fearful that something lurks in the shadows, which oft times it does.

Yes, Serena, it would be nice to live in a more human world, even for us cats. We miss the music, the dancing, the singing, and we wonder how you humans could forsake these delights for such poor fare as television.

I realize an addiction to television is not your vice, Serena, yet you still shut yourself away behind a locked door. I shall, however, wait to comment on this, for I see that your dance is ending.

· Serena ·

"Thank you," Serena said, sitting back down. "You may be the first person who's ever asked me to dance."

Michael sat on the opposite end of the window seat and stretched his legs out beside Serena's. "What? No high school prom?"

Serena shook her head. "Dancing was a no-no in my parents' church."

"God, had I known it was your first dance, I'd have first taken some lessons."

"No, it was nice."

"You're not smiling."

"It's just that it got me to thinking."

"I believe the point of dancing is not to think."

"Sorry, bad word choice. What I should have said is, it got me feeling."

"A good feeling, I hope."

Serena pushed her hair back behind one ear. "A sort of confused feeling. Dancing with you touched upon something, and now I'm feeling it well up in my solar plexus."

"Yes, I have that affect upon women. They often want to throw up."

Serena grabbed Michael's foot, and shook it. "The dance was nice, Michael, very nice. It just made me feel a phony. Here I've been talking about wanting to live in a more human world, and then you give me this chance to do something very human, something intimate, and not only am I reluctant to do it, but afterwards I feel …"

"Like you want to throw up."

"Oh, stop it! I feel … scared."

"Of me?"

"Of course not. It's something else, something…maybe I shouldn't have said 'scared.' It's just that now I'm feeling a little troubled, and when I get feeling this way, I know there's something I need to be looking at, only I'm not exactly sure what."

"Do you have to psychoanalyze everything? It was just a dance, something fun. What's the big deal?"

"But that's exactly my point. It's supposed to be fun. So why isn't it for me? What's keeping me from just letting go and going with the moment? You know the whole time we were dancing, I kept thinking of this other dream I had."

"And here I thought you were thinking how great it was to be tripping the light fantastic with the next Fred Astaire."

Serena smiled. "I wanted to be thinking that, but I kept thinking about this woman in my dream, because there was a point in the dream when she danced."

"And you're going to tell me Gerontius was with you when you had this dream."

"Of course, only I was sitting over there on the sofa."

"And where was I?"

"Probably off at some rehearsal."

Michael scooted back a little and leaned his back against the wall. "Okay, so, this is a dream about dancing?"

"Actually, it's about hatred."

Ashye's Awakening

Coriander: an aid to digestion; for aching joints; as an aphrodisiac.

I am Ashye, the fourth daughter of Ashkhan, sixth wife to Drtad, King of Armenia.

Caraway: to sweeten the breath; to relieve flatulence, though for this, verbena is better.

My father thinks of his daughters as cattle to be used as barter—so many as bribes for allegiance, so many to placate his enemies. Thank the gods, I am the one who looks most like him. My forehead is broad, my nose flat, my hair dull and limp. I am too ugly for bartering. Besides, my place is here in the garden with my herbs.

Elderflower: to smooth the skin; to sweeten wine; with yarrow for a hangover.

Each evening, just as the first stars appear in the sky, I go to the great palace hall where my father sits enthroned upon his couch, and there, kneeling before him, I bathe his stinking feet, first with a soap made from the boiled root of marsh mallow, then a soak with chamomile and hyssop. Lastly, I massage his feet with an ointment of aloe.

Then the great Drtad puts on sandals, reeking of something dead, and goes off to gorge himself on delicacies no one but he is allowed to eat. Later, he drinks the infusion of herbs I nightly prepare so his angry gut will not keep him awake.

Allium: to stimulate appetite; to cleanse the blood; for worms.

My father's is the face of war. When not plundering the land of the Persians, he amuses himself ravaging the wives of those he has slain. His taste is for women who are terrified of him; these include his wives, all sixty-two. The color of my father's urine is often angry red. Even his piss is warlike.

Chaste berry: to regulate menstruation; to assist in the passing of the afterbirth.

Perhaps I should not fault the great Drtad; the world has no meaning, so a king is justified in taking from it all he can. This I tell my cat Tamar. She yawns then goes back to rolling in the bed of catnip. I tell her she must be a Christian to show such distain for a sacred herb. Christians, in general, do not amuse me. They are dull, self-righteous prigs who would have us all prostrating ourselves before a single god–theirs, of course.

Aniseed: for colic; to increase a mother's milk; to mask the smell of death.

There is an old man, a Christian, one of their leaders. Once he and my father were friends, but when he refused to honor Anahid, our goddess, my father had this heretic cast into the pit. The old fool seemed happy to go.

That was a long time ago. By rights, the old man should be dead. Yet every day, I sneak him some bread and water. I do not go myself, for that would be too dangerous, and besides, my work with the herbs demands all my attention. My father's wives send their children to do this for me. To the children it is a game, for along with the bread, they bring rats to feed the snakes in the pit.

Why do the wives do this for me instead of betraying me to my father, for truly there is little love between any of us? It is because I make the ointment for their nipples, chapped from nursing. I make the drink which tightens their flaccid wombs. Above all, I alone know the secret of the potion that keeps a woman from again becoming pregnant. Besides, they enjoy having secrets from the king; it makes them believe they have power, though, in fact, they have none. Yet how would any of us survive if we did not convince ourselves we had power over at least one other, for power is the only thing that makes life bearable?

Which is why Gayane remains a mystery to me. She, too, was a Christian. She was also one of those women cursed with the beauty that drive men mad, which explains why my father offered to make her his first wife, above the other sixty-two. To be seated at the side of the king, would have made Gayane the most powerful woman in Armenia, perhaps the whole world.

But Gayane cared nothing for power. She only wished to live a secluded life among the sisters of her faith, all virgin brides married to the Christian god they worshipped.

When my father learned of this, he showed restraint not in keeping with his nature. Instead of forcing Gayane into marriage, he sent her a gift, a magnificent stallion, seventeen hands high, yet so gentle, a lady need not fear to ride him.

I was envious, for I have always wanted a horse, if only an old nag, useful for carrying baskets of herbs. Yet Gayane sent back the stallion along with this message: Trade not the joys and pleasures of heaven for the glories of this world.

I was there the morning my father received this, for I'd been summoned to treat his corns, which were making him hobble about like an old cripple. I saw that my father was truly bewitched, for instead of having Gayane killed for her insolence, he sent her another present, a robe made from leopard skins.

This Gayane also returned.

Again, and again, my father sent offerings, each one more magnificent than the last, and each time Gayane sent them back and always with the same message: Trade not the joys and pleasures of heaven for the glories of this world.

Finally, when his twelfth gift was rejected, my father's wrath filled him as fire fills a burning house, and he ordered his soldiers to fetch Gayane by force. They entered the community of sisters and killed all save Gayane, whom they bound with ropes and brought back, dragged behind their horses. And there in the great square where all could see, my father unleashed his men, and they set upon Gayane as ravenous dogs upon a helpless lamb.

I had no wish to see this spectacle, yet I learned firsthand what befell Gayane, for by means within my power, I recovered her body and set about preparing it for burial. I cannot bring myself to tell of all the outrages inflicted upon her. I will only say that in washing her body, I found very few bones not broken. To my surprise, her face was almost untouched, though this may have been so ordered by my father.

I washed the body then laid it upon fresh linen and packed it around with aromatic herbs, bringing the cloth up around the body as I worked. Then I wound the cloth with strips of linen, until Gayane was a caterpillar within her own chrysalis with only her face visible. Often, I caught myself staring at that face. I have seen more people who have died by the hand of violence then I care to count. Their faces are either contorted in fear, or glassy-eyed, dull, uncomprehending. Yet the face of Gayane appeared peaceful and content, with the corner of her lips drawn into a small smile. Given the manner of her death, the smile puzzled me. Was it her way of having the last say with her tormentors, or had Gayane, in the moment before her spirit departed her body, actually beheld those pleasures of heaven she had traded her earthly life for? Had her benevolent god waited with hand outstretched to draw her up to a place beside him?

Milk vetch: to relieve bloating; for fatigue; for night sweats.

Since Gayane's death, my mind has given me no peace, not even in sleep wherein I dream of Gayane's smiling face. My understanding of the world has always been as something solid, a wall as unassailable as those that surround my father's palace. Now I see that my wall has cracks, and I know of no way of patching them. This torments me, leaves me weak, and makes all I have to do that much harder. I have spoken of power as that which makes life bearable. The power of a woman has always been as water, whereas men are stones—hard, unyielding, unmovable—and we must content ourselves with flowing around them. Yet given time, water can wear away stone.

Damiana: for bad complexion; to ease breathing; for headaches when menstruating.

My father, the great Drtad, has fallen ill. Some say he has become possessed of demons, for he goes about like a wild beast, howling and frothing at the mouth. Others say a sister to Gayane, one who managed to escape the slaughter, has called upon the powers of her god to place a curse upon him. There is even a rumor that my father's sickness is the result of a stricken conscious, which only proves that whoever has spread this rumor knows nothing of my father.

Those nearest to the king suspect he is being poisoned, though how and by what means they do not know, for the king is now kept hidden away behind stout doors, which are guarded day and night. The only exception is when he makes his visits to the house of his wives, for it seems his affliction has done nothing to lessen his appetite for women. There are some who fear the wives themselves are poisoning the king, though in truth, they are surprisingly gentle with him, bathing the sores on his hands and feet, rubbing ointment on his skin rashes and oils on his aching muscles.

Of course, I prepare all these ointments, only now I have to prove them safe, and knowing my affection for my cat Tamar, my father's advisors make me first test them upon her.

Valerian: for insomnia; for melancholy; to control trembling.

Increasingly. my father has to be restrained lest in his violent fits he might do himself injury. Then he strains against his bonds, spits curses, snaps his teeth until, exhausted, he falls to the floor and lies there, weeping. Only then can I force upon him a calming drink. Out of desperation, my father's advisors have abandoned our gods in favor of faith healers and religious zealots of every stripe, men who claim to have the power to drive out demons. Old fools! I could have told them these snivelers and posers can do my father no good.

Then someone remembered the Christian who had been cast into the pit. Perhaps, if he still lived, he might be prevailed upon to aid my father. Considering my father's treatment of Christians, I think this folly, but of course, no one asks me my thoughts. The old man is hauled up out of the pit, and I am given the task of cleaning him up. It takes the better part of a day to scrub the filth off him. I also treat his sores and feed him broths, for he is emaciated. In the course of ministering to him, I learn his name. He is Gregory of Caesarea, a city in Cappadocia. Judging Gregory clean enough, I bring him to my father's chamber, whereupon seeing my father, who lies upon the floor crying, Gregory begins to cry also.

"My friend," Gregory says, "how it grieves me to see you like this. Yet were you not warned that the wages of sin are death, not only here, but also in the hereafter?" Then Gregory places a hand upon my father's forehead and begins to pray. Fortunately for him, my father has not the fit upon him, otherwise that hand likely would be bitten. Gregory is a long time praying, hours it seems. Tired of listening, I doze off in the corner of the room where I have been watching. It is Gregory who wakes me. "Come," he says, and I follow as we pass out of my father's chamber and into the garden where we will not be disturbed.

"Sit," Gregory commands, pointing to bench beside the pool of water. But I am not about to take orders from one still smelling of muck.

"Tell me, what of my father? Will he live?"

Gregory shrugs. "Surely, there are those who have died who deserved to live, and many have lived who deserved death. Your father's life is in the hands of God, and God's ways are mysterious."

"You talk riddles, old man."

Gregory smiles. It is not a good smile, for many of his teeth have fallen out. Yet there is kindness in it. "I do not know if King Drtad will live or die. But why should you care? You love him not."

I draw myself up to full height. "How dare you speak to me like that. I am a princess, of royal blood."

"I only speak the truth as God gives me to see it. I will tell you what I once told your father: 'I fear not your high and mighty ways, for they are as nothing to Him.'" He lifts a finger skyward.

Then Gregory surprises me by taking my hands in his. I try to pull away, but he possesses uncommon strength. "Look at me," he commands.

Meekly, I obey. His eyes seem to look past mine until I feel he is staring in upon my very soul. I squirm beneath that stare, yet he holds me fast. He seems something other than a man, rather an angel standing in judgment. Without knowing the reason, I begin to cry.

Gregory releases me. I step back, take a deep breath, shake my head to clear it. When I dare look again at Gregory, I see just an old man with tears running alongside his scabrous nose. Somehow I know those tears are for me. Then he places a gentle hand upon my cheek. Ugly as I am, I have never been looked upon with love by a man, not that Gregory sees me with a lover's eyes; his love is that of a father for a daughter, something I have experienced but once, and that in a dream, whereupon I awoke, weeping.

"Release him, my child," Gregory says. "For the sake of your mortal soul, release your father and let him live."

Club moss: for urinary infections; for constipation; for itching.

My father's advisors allow Gregory considerable freedom, letting him come and go as he pleases. I sense they fear him, for how is it possible for a man to have survived so long in the pit? When my father is not in one of his violent fits, Gregory prays over him. I know, for I watch from the shadows. I want to see if Gregory's powers extend to healing the sick. His talents appear limited to prayer. Granted, he has a great ability in this. Gregory can pray for hours on end and never tire. Yet for all the good his prayers do my father, Gregory might just as well be spending his time standing on his head. I draw great satisfaction from this, for it affirms my power over his.

And what is my power? If power were something one could throw into a cooking pot, mine would boil down to one thing: hate. I hate my father who was a beast long before he started to howl like one. I hate him for what he did to poor Gayane. But most of all, I hate my father because he has never looked at me, never touched me, never spoken my name. I am a king's daughter, yet share not in my father's kingdom. To my father, I am less than a slave. I am a dropping, the discharge from a place where he once stuck in his penis.

There are those who say hate is an inferior power. They are fools. There is nothing to equal the pleasure of seeing the man I hate made to suffer and cry out in fear and pain, and to know that I am the cause of it, and, furthermore that I, Ashye, fourth daughter of Ashkhan, hold in my hand the power of life and death over a king.

Yet, there are times when I would gladly trade all my power to be looked upon, just once, with love by my father.

Angelica: for seasickness; to freshen the air; to protect against evil.

"If I do as you wish, what will you give me in return?"

Gregory appears not to have heard my question. His attention is upon Tamar, and I am now sorry I did not find a place other than my herb garden for us to talk. Tamar is rubbing against his leg. Her loud purr tells me she is hungry.

Yet when I go to lift her up, she escapes my fingers and instead hops up on Gregory's lap. My displeasure is not lost upon him. He briefly scratches Tamar's head then holds her out for me to take. The swiftness with which I take her, reveals my jealousy. I set Tamar upon the wall beside me and feed her tidbits left over from my meal.

"You ask what it is I can give you," Gregory says. "I can give you nothing, child, but were I able to give you everything you want, I would not, for there is nothing you want that is good."

His words are a slap in the face. "What do you know of what I want? Who are *you*, old man, to judge *me*?"

Gregory looks very tired. "You are your father's child, so very much like him."

I spit at his feet. "I am nothing like my father. He is a beast."

"Ah, but you both think alike. You see what is least in a man: his selfishness, his greed, his lust for the things of this world, even his fears, and then you turn these evils against him in order to increase your own power. But as I told your father when he offered to spare my life if I would but worship your false gods: 'God, the one true God, does not barter.'"

"Do not be so scornful of power. It was because of my power that you live."

"It is by the will of God that I live!"

I shake my head. "Who do you think fed you, there in the pit?"

Gregory looks surprised. "That was you?"

With a feeling of triumph, I nod.

"Then I am grateful to you. Your bread helped ease the suffering of many."

Now I am the one surprised. "You did not eat the bread I gave you?"

"Some, yes, but did you not think there were others in the pit? Their need was as great as mine."

I hate this man. I see why my father had him cast into the pit. And then I realize that perhaps I am not so unlike my father after all.

Agrimony: to dye cloth yellow; for disorders of the eye.

This is the worst my father has ever been. He is truly a demon, possessed with a demon's strength. The guards are frightened, and I know what they are thinking. They wonder if the chain that binds my father to the wall will hold. With each furious pull, the wall shudders, and when the ringbolt does not give, my father raves and spits curses at us.

I, too, am frightened. There is fire in my father's eyes, and when he turns them upon me, I feel a burning, and for some reason I cannot explain, I wish Gregory were here.

Then I see him out of the corner of my eye. He has entered my father's chamber, holding Tamar. Before I can react, Gregory walks right up to my father and hands Tamar to him. I scream and rush forward, but stop just short of my father's outstretched arms. I do not know what to do. I'm too frightened to go forward, yet the only thing I have ever loved is in the arms of the beast.

My father snaps his teeth at me, like a dog warning me off his bone, only the bone is Tamar. I feel so helpless. The gods are laughing at me. I swear by all of them, I will kill Gregory. I do not understand why Tamar does not try to save herself. Where are her claws, her teeth? Her eyes are half-lidded as when she rolls about in catnip.

I look to my father and see that the fire has gone out of his eyes, and the fury no longer possesses him. My father's hand, which could easily crush a cat's skull, hovers over Tamar's head, lightly caressing it. His fingers find the spot where Tamar most likes to be scratched, just behind her nose. Tamar pushes her head upward against those fingers. She is purring is as loud as when she is hungry.

My father smiles and laughs a little. The laugh confuses me. I do not know what to do. I should use this moment to rescue my Tamar, yet my feet are stuck to the floor. Then there is a hand upon my back, and I am roughly shoved forward, and I find myself face to face with my father. His eyes are unnaturally bright, and I wonder if the fit is about to take him again.

My father brings his arm up, the one not cradling Tamar, and rubs his hand lightly along my cheek.

"Ashye," he says.

His saying my name is an arrow piercing my black heart, and all the venom pours out to join my tears, which are now raining down upon the floor.

"Ashye, my daughter."

Thyme: for coughs and sore throat; in a bath to increase strength and courage.

My father is getting better, and I am certain he will soon be as well as ever. My father's advisors say it is a miracle and give Gregory the credit. This confirms what I have always known about men: being of stone they think like a stone, with minds just as unyielding. Men assume that death comes about through action: the viper's bite, the well-placed sword, a calculated poison. They fail to understand that death can just as easily result from actions withheld as taken, for example, the withholding of a common herb or two from an infusion to aid digestion, the absence of which causes certain men, afflicted with a rare disease, to go mad.

Yet I care not that Gregory gets the credit, for my father is a changed man, and to me, that is the true miracle. Whereas before my father brought war, he now brings peace. To those who felt the bite of his anger, he now touches with kindness. To those wronged, he seeks to make amends.

My father is building a church. I do not mean that my father has ordered a church to be built. I mean that *he* is building the church, using his great strength to set the stones in place. It is joyous work. I know, for I am always at his side, helping to lift. He is building his church on the ground where the sisters of poor Gayane were murdered, and when it is done, Gregory will preach there of his Christian God, and we will be the first of his congregation.

There is so much that I do not understand about this new religion, and many of Gregory's explanations are not helpful. He thinks too much. I only know what I feel. I used to feel hate, a hate so strong I was fooled into thinking I possessed a great power. I know now that hatred has no master; hated and hater are alike destroyed. Whereas love, which is what I feel now, nourishes all. Love is everywhere I look, but most of all in the faces of those I love: Tamar, Gregory, my father.

Gregory says that God is love, and I believe it, for I felt His hand upon me that awful day when Gregory placed poor Tamar into the hands of my demented father. I thought it was Gregory who pushed me forward, but he swears he did not touch me. I know now it was God, His hand in the small of my back, shoving me forward to face my father. Then He took from me my hatred and awakened in me love, I who so little deserve it.

But enough! The long day with the heavy stones is ending. We are tired, my father and I, yet happy. Our happiness makes us silly, and so, amid the foundations of what I know will one day be a great church, we join hands, father and daughter, and with God smiling down upon us, we dance.

Arnica: for sprains and bruises; to relieve muscle soreness.

· Serena ·

"You're right, Serena," Michael said, "that dream was definitely not about dancing."

"No," Serena said, "it was about someone who was deeply hurt by her father."

"So, what does this dream have to do with you? Was your father abusive?"

"Absolutely not! My father's a very kind and loving man. He was always strict with my sister and me, but in no way abusive. In fact, I can't ever remember being spanked."

"So what happened? You got the wrong dream?"

Serena brushed her hair back. "No, this dream was meant for me. It gives me that feeling I was telling you about, the one coming from my solar plexus."

"I think that's called a gut-level feeling, Serena."

Serena smiled. "Sorry, I guess I've always been a bit prim. But 'gut' is the word for it, and my gut tells me that this dream is saying something specifically about me, only, I'm not exactly sure what. I was hoping you could help me figure it out."

Michael scratched his cheek. "Well, you already know I'm no Sigmund Freud, but as I was listening, I kept noticing a recurring image, that of walls. The woman, Ashye, lived within the palace walls, and nowhere does it say she ever went out of them, not even to go to the square to see Gayane being murdered. She seemed to go only two places: her garden, which I imagine was surrounded by walls in order to keep animals out, and the palace, where she went to take care of her father. She didn't even go to the snake pit to give Gregory bread, but sent children. To top it off, she used the word 'wall' to describe how she saw the world."

"I think the image of a wall must represent her bottled up emotions," Serena said. "It was a symbol for the hatred she hid from others lest she be punished for it."

Michael shook his head. "I believe it represents something quite straight forward. Let's go back to what we were talking about earlier: the seven deadly sins. You said my sin was acedia. Well, it seems to me this dream is saying acedia is your sin, too."

"And you got that from 'walls'? Excuse me, but I'm going to need a bit more convincing."

"Okay, bear with me on this because I'm sort of thinking this through as I go along. Didn't you say that acedia was the monk's sin?"

"It wasn't limited to monks, but supposedly monks often committed it."

"And what comes to mind when you think of monks?"

"Michael, why don't you just tell me what you're getting at?"

"Humor me. What do you think when you hear the word 'monk'?"

"I think of someone who's very devout. Someone who believes that matters of spirit are more important than earthly delights. Someone who directs all his efforts toward knowing God."

"You know what I think of when I hear the word 'monk'? I think of walls. I think of the Spanish missions with their massive, six-foot thick walls. I think of bell walls. I think of old men copying script, or shuffling along to mass, or sitting in cells fingering their rosaries, all the while surrounded by walls."

"I don't think you'd find any of that representative of present-day monks."

"I'm not talking about present-day monks. I'm talking about repeating images. I guess it's my musical training, but I tend to look for themes. I may not be very good with subtle philosophical distinctions, but I know a theme when I come across it."

"And that's how you see me, as someone who lives behind walls?"

"I'm afraid I do."

"But I'm not Ashye. I'm not consumed with hate. I'd never dream of killing my father."

"You don't have to hate someone to live behind walls. Monks live behind walls."

Serena drew her knees to her chest and began to rock a little.

"Have I offended you?" Michael said.

"No, I'm just trying to see if what you just said resonates with my gut feeling. I'm still not sure what this has to do with me and acedia."

"Okay, let me go on. You said my sin was acedia because I criticize everything, because I'm negative, because I don't believe in much of anything."

"I think I said those things because you were being really irritating at the time."

"Come on, Serena, don't start back peddling now. I admit there's some truth in what you said, but can't the same thing be said of you? What was it you said earlier? You feel like you don't belong here, that you were born in the wrong time. You said that nowadays people are only out for themselves—they're angry, pushy, self-centered, and you want nothing to do with them. You'd rather hide away here in your room." Michael points to the book Serena left lying near the window seat. "Who was that monk you quoted earlier?"

"You mean Cassian?"

"Didn't he say that a monk whose sin is acedia is someone who thinks he'd be better off in another monastery where everything is ..."

Serena picked up the book and read aloud. " 'He dwells much on the excellence of other and distant monasteries. He thinks how profitable and healthy life is there, how delightful the brethren are, and how spiritually they talk.' "

"Right! Doesn't that describe you perfectly? Don't you have this fantasy of living in some quaint country village where everyone looks out for each other?" Michael lifted his hands toward the ceiling. "O ye gods, transport Serena back to the middle ages, where everything is idyllic!"

"But Cassian was describing a monk who was basically apathetic toward life," Serena said.

"And what are you?"

"I'm not apathetic. I'm frightened. Look, Michael, you're a man, you're bigger, stronger. For you, the world's not as threatening."

"I'm not so sure I agree with that. No matter who you are, there's always someone bigger."

"But there's more to it than that. Despite some recent historic changes, it's still very much a man's world."

"I still don't agree."

"Listen for a moment. I'm not talking about the number of women working today as CEOs. I'm talking about something far more primitive. Engulfing this world is an atmosphere of aggression. Just pick up any newspaper: wars, genocide, rape, torture. And who are committing these atrocities? Men! Ninety-nine-point-nine percent of the time, it's men! We live in a world where men use violence to force their will upon others. And what can we women do about it? Take them on? Go at them with guns and knives? Even if we chose to do something so horrible, we'd lose. Ashye was right: men are stones, and we women must be content with trying to flow around them and hope we don't get crushed."

"And that's why you sit at home alone, so you won't be crushed?"

Serena shut the book and hugged it to her chest. "Do you think I'd be afraid to go out at night if there were only women out there?"

Michael leaned back against the wall and stared at the ceiling.

"I hope you know, Michael, that when I'm talking about men as aggressors, I'm not talking about you." When Michael didn't reply, she added, "It's very late. Maybe we should finish this discussion another time."

Michael shook his head. "You know, earlier, you came at me pretty hard. You said I could twist my arrogance around and make it sound like a virtue. Well, now I feel I need to tell you a few things you might find hard to hear. You say you fear the world, and I understand that. I get pretty frightened sometimes, myself. But being afraid doesn't let you off the hook. Whether you're someone like me, who sins out of arrogance, or someone like you, who sins out of fear, it's still acedia."

"But you—"

"Just listen. You know the hard part of hearing what you said about me earlier? Well, two things, really. The first was being told something I didn't want to hear: that I'm this jerk who criticizes everything and doesn't see the good in anything."

"I didn't say 'jerk.'"

"Well, I just did, because the more I think about it the more I realize it's true, and that gets me to the second part, the really tough part, because once I accept the fact that I'm this negative person, then that pretty much compels me to do something about it."

"Which only shows how much of a good person you are."

"Thank you. The same can be said of you, which is why you can't give in to fear."

"But have you ever been really and truly frightened, Michael?"

"Yes, believe it or not, I have, and let me tell you, it's no fun. And what makes it worse is the way the fear lingers on in your mind and colors the way you look at things. Which brings me to the point I'm trying to make. I don't really know much about your past, but I get the feeling that fear has done that to you—colored the way you look at things, otherwise you wouldn't see the world so fearfully. You may not think me the best judge, but I say there's a lot of good out there. There are a lot of good people doing a lot of good things, and if you wish to free yourself from acedia, you're going to have to be more a part of this world."

Serena was quiet for so long Michael started to feel uneasy. "I can't tell by you silences whether you're just thinking, or plotting to bombard me with caramels."

Serena smiled. "I reserve caramels for chastising those who are truly disagreeable."

"Uh-oh, should I run for cover?"

"No, Michael. If you've been disagreeable, it's because you've said something I needed to hear, but didn't want to."

"So, my comments resonated with your gut feeling?"

Serena smoothed down a crease in her skirt. "Yes and no."

"I'll take that to mean I'm batting five hundred."

"It means you're batting a thousand. I'm just not sure what the game is."

Michael grinned. "God, Serena, you make everything so complicated."

"Well, I'm sorry if I'm not one of those people who sees everything as black or white."

"I didn't mean that as a criticism. I like the fact that you're complicated. It makes you interesting."

"Interesting or strange?"

Michael squeezed Serena's foot. "Strangely interesting."

"Should I take that as a compliment?"

"Yes! Now, was there anything else about your dream that spoke to you."

"First, let me ask you what you thought of the ending."

"Very contrived. God reaches out, literally, and miraculously makes everything hunky-dory between Ashye and her father."

"Hunky-dory?"

"Technical psychological jargon."

"So, you don't believe in miracles?"

"Do you?"

Serena was a while thinking. "Yes and no." She laughed. "There I go again being strangely interesting."

"Does that mean that you can't answer the question?"

Serena thought some more. "I think the ending of my dream should perhaps be taken as a metaphor."

"Very Freudian."

"Hush! Let me go back to what Ashye said earlier in my dream, that she would gladly trade all her power to be looked upon, just once, with love by her father. She had this deep wound that could only be healed by her father's love."

"Which father, her earthly father or her heavenly one?"

"I suspect both. For some reason, that brings to mind an experience I had when I was a part of a therapy group. The group leader asked us to participate in a two-part exercise where we first had to write down as many 'wants' as we could in two minutes while she played excerpts of pop songs with lyrics about wanting things."

"What do you mean by 'wants.'"

"You know, materialistic stuff: money, a nice car, a house on the beach in Malibu. The idea was to be playful, to imagine what it would be like if we won the lottery and could have anything we wanted. But what was interesting was the second part of the exercise. While we listened to some really evocative piece of music, we had to write down what we *really* wanted out of life. You see, the first part of the exercise was to flush out our superficial desires in order to get at what we really wanted deep inside."

"I'd like to know what music she played for the second part. I could think of quite a few pieces I would have chosen."

"I've no idea what the music was, but it was very moving."

"So, what was your deep psychological insight? What did you write down?"

Serena took in a deep breath and slowly released it.

"What?" Michael said.

"I think I may have just figured out what my gut has been trying to tell me."

· Gerontius ·

Brava! Serena, for finally getting to the source of your gut feeling, though I'm not surprised since you've always been very introspective, as evidenced by the time you spend meditating. I've spied you sitting cross-legged on your cushion, eyes closed, your chest slowly rising and falling in response to your measured breathing. I particularly cherish those summer days when you left your window open to the breeze, allowing me to slip into your apartment and curl up on your legs as you sit in repose. There is no better place more conducive for a restful nap than on the lap of someone at perfect peace.

Would that Michael could learn from you. His mind is a whirligig. Snippets of thoughts—unknowable futures, past regrets—go spinning about in his mental cavity, yet never go anywhere. The only time he stays focused longer than the time it takes him to gobble a caramel is when he's immersed in some pleasant reverie usually having to do with sex.

Thank goodness, we cats are not so cursed. Why should we waste our mental energies on "what ifs" or "if onlys" when there are majestic trees to climb and succulent gophers to munch and forlorn humans to guide over the bumps of life? As for sex, we don't rhapsodize over it, we just do it, at least those who haven't had the misfortune of being introduced to a veterinarian.

But you, dear Serena, are like an early explorer, only your dark continent is the inner realm. Embarked upon a particular river of thought, you stay with it through twisting and turnings and false tributaries, going deeper and deeper into the subcontinent until you arrive at the water's source and the secret to be found there.

I'm most anxious to hear what you've discovered about your gut feeling, though I sense you may be reluctant to share your discovery with Michael.

• Serena •

"So, what has your gut been telling you?" Michael said. "And what does it have to do with the group therapy exercise?"

"Do you really want to hear this?" Serena said. "It will take some explaining, and even then, I don't know if it will make that much sense."

"Try me."

"Okay, the group therapy thing was obviously about discovering what we really wanted in life."

"So, what did you write down?"

"I think I wrote that I wanted to be happy."

"A popular choice. I'd have gone with 'being rich.'"

Serena smiled. "The thing is, I remember being very moved by the music. It was very ethereal and seemed to take me to someplace deep inside, a place of yearning, only I couldn't quite figure out what it was that I was yearning for. And up until just a minute ago, it was the same with my dream about Ashye."

"So what is it you just discovered?"

"To answer, I'm going to have to digress a bit."

Michael smiled. "Why am I not surprised?"

"Do you want to hear this or not?"

"I'm all ears."

"Okay, first let me ask you a question. Who are you?"

"Oh God, a philosophical question. Well, I'm not a philosopher. I'm a musician, so all I need to know about who I am is that I'm Michael and I sing."

"Is that it? Is that all you are?"

Michael looked at Gerontius, resting on Serena's lap. "Are you listening to this Gerontius? It's the middle of the night, and Serena is wanting me to have to think." Michael leaned back and momentarily closed his eyes. "To answer your question as best as I can under conditions of limited mental functioning, I'd say I am the product of all my experiences as they were shaped by my environment."

"So, you are nothing more than a collection of experiences?"

"What else is there?"

"What about your innate abilities?"

"Okay, I'll add my genes. Genes plus experience plus environment equals Michael."

Serena sat a while thinking.

"What?" Michael said. "You don't like my answer?"

"No, Michael, it is a very good answer, one I think most scientists and some philosophers would agree with."

"But you don't."

"I guess I'm wanting to think I'm more than a grab bag of assorted genes, experiences and environments."

"You mean something like a soul?"

"I mean genes, experiences and reactions to environments are just accommodations that allow me to function in the material world. They are not who I am."

"Okay, so who are you then?"

Serena moved Gerontius from her lap to a place beside her. "When I was just a child, I was taught a Bible verse that began, 'For God so loved the world that he gave his only begotten son.' I've always been intrigued by that word 'begotten.'"

"I'm interested in who it was God was begetting?" Michael said.

"That's an interesting point. According to Luke, God placed his seed in a poor commoner, a woman who was little more than a child. That means that Jesus, who was the product of that begetting, was the union of heaven and earth, of the divine and the mundane. Yet repeatedly, Jesus said that the seed of God was in each of us as well.

He illustrated this with the parable of the mustard seed, which is the smallest of seeds, but when allowed to grow, becomes a shrub big enough for birds to nest under. So, getting back to the earlier question of what it is I want, I want to find this seed of God within me, for I sense it is who I truly am, and all the other flotsam and jetsam of existence—my experiences, my thoughts and emotions, and certainly, my beliefs and opinions—are just distractions, preventing my seed from growing. That was Ashye's problem. Her father's indifference and his cruelty, combined with her loneliness, were experiences that made her a very hateful person. But that wasn't who she truly was, and it wasn't until she felt a godlike presence, or to put it another way, until she found the seed of god within herself, that she became free of hatred and, as a consequence, filled with joy. The Buddhists know all this very well. The Buddha said that our likes and dislikes, our thoughts and opinions, our obsessions with the past and the future are all illusions, masking who we truly are."

Michael sighed. "You, Serena, are a seeker. Me, I'm just a common, run-of-the-mill kind of guy. All I know is that I'm a singer."

"But I don't think a seeker and a singer are that far apart. The Buddha said the goal of seeking is to find freedom from illusion and realize the joy of liberation. Listening to you singing tonight, I sensed that freedom within you. It seemed you gave yourself over to nothing other than bringing beauty and meaning to the role of Gerontius. Surely, that must have given you joy."

Michael grinned. "Well, now that you mention it, I was a bit pleased." He laughed. "What do you know, I'm a goddamn Buddha."

"Speaking of singing, you've had a long night. You must be exhausted."

"Actually, I'm just feeling relaxed."

"In that case, would you care to hear another one of my dreams?"

"Is this another religious one?"

"No, it's about a rat."

The Tragedy of Cawdallor, the Rat King

When Pope Gregory IX, that crusty old inquisitor, issued a Papal Bull declaring cats "diabolical creatures," it began what came to be known as the Golden Age of Rats. Thousands, nay hundreds of thousands, of cats, were put to the torch. The rats, amazed by this sudden turn of events, sat upon rooftops and brick piles and cast off wine barrels to watch as their old archenemies were consigned to the flames.

"Wonderful!" they declared, firelight dancing in their liquid brown eyes. "Delightful! About time, too!"

Yet little did Gregory realize the possible consequence of his edict, for, as we now know, cats prey upon rats, who harbor fleas, which carry the plague, which kills people. Suddenly a person's sniffle wasn't just the start of another summer cold, and it wasn't long before the bodies began to pile up. Yet as they say, "One man's poison is another man's meat," or, as the rats put it, "Don't dither! Start munching on a liver!"

For the rats, it got even better, for soon there was no longer enough people to harvest the crops, and food was free for the taking, provided the rats could get past the scavenging dogs. That's when Cawdallor the Rat King organized the rats into militias, and in swift, furious battles, they either slew the dogs or drove them from the fields, bloody tails dangling between their legs. Then came a time of such drinking and feasting and merrymaking as never had been seen amongst rats, and nowhere merrier than in King Cawdallor's court. In his great dining hall, where the mice waited upon the rats, no plate was ever empty, no goblet fully drained. The rats ate until they could eat no more, ate until their tummies were tight as tins, ate until they were exhausted and fell asleep right there at the tables, often sleeping right through the nightly entertainments, which is where I, Teig, a cat, came in.

"Got a bit of something special for you tonight, sire," said Twllyn, the rat-captain of the guard, as he leaned upon the back of the great throne whereupon sat Cawdallor, a platter of the best victuals by his paw.

"Not more flea races, I hope, Twllyn."

"No, sire."

"No, 'Who Cut the Cheese?'"

"No, sire."

"Last time, it took a week to air the place out."

"Yes, sire."

Cawdallor popped a grape into his mouth. "So what's it to be? I rather liked it when the guards raced about on those little wire wheels."

"Nothing like that, sire. This time we got us a cat."

Cawdallor inhaled a whole grape.

"There, there," Twllyn said, thumping the king on the back. "Never you worry, my lord. We've got this one good and beaten down."

Cawdallor hawked up the grape and spat it out on the floor. "My god, Twllyn, what are you planning?"

Twllyn grinned. "I thought we'd make him run the gauntlet, sire. You know, up and down the hall while we poke things at him."

"Excellent!" Cawdallor cried, banging his paw on the arm of his throne. "That ought to wake up these slugs! By all means, Twllyn, bring in this cat of yours."

Then with a fanfare of trumpets, I was dragged forward by two columns of rats, pulling on ropes tied about my neck.

"Well, well, look what the rats dragged in," Cawdallor said.

Though tempted, I figured this was no time for snappy comebacks, and in fairness, I did look miserable, so miserable I think even Cawdallor, not known for a soft heart, felt a bit sorry for me. I have always been of middling size, but look bigger due to the length and thickness of my fine black fur. But months of dodging the inquisition had taken its toll. My hair was falling out in clumps. One of my ears was torn from an earlier tangle with a gang of marauding dogs, and several of my whiskers were missing.

"How do you expect him to run?" Cawdallor said, pointing, for it was obvious I was favoring my right front paw, which had been injured during my capture.

"Oh, we'll get him to run all right," Twllyn said, nodding toward the entryway where two guards appeared, each bearing a burning torch.

There was a look of alarm on Cawdallor face. "You're going to use fire? Are you sure this is such a good idea, Twllyn? And I don't suppose you've figured out what you're going to do with the cat once you're through with him?"

Twllyn cleared his throat. Obviously, he hadn't. "I suppose, sire, we could kill him and eat him."

Cawdallor hawked and spat. "We both know cats are all bone and gristle."

"Or we could give him to a dog." Twllyn said.

Cawdallor drummed his digits on the arm of his chair. "Bring the cat closer. I want to talk to him."

Twllyn signaled the guards, and they pulled me towards the throne. "Greetings, O Rat King," I said.

Twllyn smacked my injured paw with his staff. "Bow before His Majesty, you filthy dog, I mean cat!"

But bowing was impossible with the ropes taut about my neck.

"Ease off!" Cawdallor commanded. The soldiers let the ropes go slack.

"Thank you, Your Majesty," I said, bending my head so my nose nearly touched the floor.

"Come closer," Cawdallor commanded.

I limped forward.

"What's your name, cat?"

"My name is Teig, Your Majesty."

Twllyn snorted. "Sounds short for tiger. You cats are always coming up with poofed-up names."

"No, good sir," I said, fixing Twllyn with one of my yellow eyes. "Teig means poet."

"And what the hell's a poet?" Twllyn said.

"Hush, Twllyn," Cawdallor commanded.

But I went ahead and answered the question. "A poet is an artist with words. Perhaps you've read some of my poems, Your Majesty, 'Cat at My Window, Window Cat,' 'How Like the Winter Hath My Abscess Been,' 'Elegy Written in a Country Cathouse'? Then there's my epic poem, *Kubla Kat*."

"Read!" Twllyn exclaimed. "The king's a warrior, not some poofed-up scholar."

Cawdallor smoothed back his whiskers. "These poems of yours, Teig, can you recite any?"

"Of course, Your Majesty. Here's one of my favorites:

Because I could not stop for Dinner,
He kindly stopped for me;
The —

"Wait!" Cawdallor cried, pounding his scepter on the floor. "Can you make up one of these poems on the spot?"

I inclined my head. "Of course, Your Majesty."

"Then, look about my grand palace," Cawdallor said, with a sweep of his paw. "Everything you see, save the stone walls, has been fashioned from the remains of our feasts. The floor tiles were quarried from human pelvic bones and inlayed with genuine kidney stones. Finger bones were used to make the tables and chairs, which you may notice have been upholstered in genuine moustache hair. The chandeliers were fashioned from belt buckles, wedding bands and bits of eye glasses, and are lit with candles made of ear wax. My palace is truly a magnificent edifice, so, give us a poem and make it about the splendors you see before you."

I looked about. It was not 'splendors' that were most apparent to the eye, but rather a scene of revelry spent. The rats slept, face down in their plates. The mice, weary from shouldering the heavy trays, stumbled over the uneven flooring, and cockroaches swarmed over the tables, gobbling up spilled food.

"Hmm," I said, clearing my throat. "Ah." My tail twitched of its own accord.

"He can't do it, sire," Twylln said. "How about the gauntlet?"

Cawdallor raised a paw. "Patience, Twllyn. Give him a chance."

"I think, if Your Majesty would permit," I said, "I might attempt a sonnet. Let's see …

> *Shall I compare a palace to a tree?*
> *Can sapless stone be joined with swelling reed?*
> *For life is flora's commonality,*
> *And never was there stone that grew from seed.*
> *Yet might we stand amidst the wand'ring stars*
> *To measure time with Kronos' six-fold eyes,*
> *We'd gauge the Titan's sweep as little far,*
> *And in that twinkling all things live and die.*
> *For beneath the globe of heaven's lustrous crown,*
> *The gnomon marks the path from birth to death.*
> *Its shadow casts the lofty mountain down,*
> *And grinds all stone till naught but dust is left.*
> *Thus, as sure as night, as certain as the day,*
> *Your palace, O Mighty King, shall also pass away.*

Twllyn thumped his staff on the floor. "I don't like the tone of that one bit. Perhaps, Teig, you'd sing a different tune if we fed you to the dogs." Twylln turned to Cawdallor. "What say you, sire?"

Cawdallor, deep in thought, did not reply.

"Your Majesty?" Twllyn said.

"Twllyn, leave us."

"But sire, what about the cat?"

"Leave, and take the guards with you!" Cawdallor shouted. "And get those damned ropes off our guest!"

When this was done, Cawdallor motioned for me to join him. "I'm sorry I've no chair to accommodate your size."

"That's quite all right, Your Majesty," I said. "If you don't mind, I'll just stretch out here at your feet."

"Have you had anything to eat?"

"I confess I've not eaten in days."

"Bring my guest some fish!" Cawdallor ordered. "And a large bowl of milk."

Cawdallor waited until I'd eaten and washed up before resuming conversation. "Do you think I could learn to write a poem?" he said.

"Can Your Majesty write?"

"Oh," Cawdallor said, his shoulders slumping. "Yes, well… I'd not thought of that." He then straightened up. "But I could make up a poem, couldn't I, the way just you did? That was very clever, by the way."

"Thank you, Your Majesty. I've worked long to develop the skill."

"How long?"

"Many, many years, stretching back to when I was just a kitten."

"Oh," Cawdallor said, his shoulders slumping again. "Then I suppose I'd be a very old rat, indeed, before I got the knack."

I looked about to see if any rats were listening. There was only Twllyn, out of earshot, but with his eye fixed on me. "Your Majesty, might I speak freely?"

"Yes, of course."

I leaned in close. "I've a pretty good sense of where a creature's talents lie, and though I don't doubt in time you would produce some very excellent poems, I believe poetry is not your medium."

"So what you're really saying, Teig, in a nice sort of way, is that I've no talent."

"Not at all, Your Majesty. When I first saw you, I said to myself, 'Now there is a rat who is a true artist.'"

"Really?" Cawdallor said, sitting up tall and preening his whiskers. "Uh, what's an artist?"

"An artist, sire, is someone who sees the world differently. He senses there is another reality—behind that which we see—another world, you might say. It is the artist's job to express himself in such a way that this other reality becomes evident to those who cannot see it. This often makes the artist disliked, even hated, for this new reality is often in opposition to the old, and to those who are firmly attached to the old reality, this new reality seems quite threatening." I lifted a paw. "Am I making myself clear, sire?"

"Yes, I think so." Cawdallor tapped his chin with a finger. "I think I owe my throne, in part, to this 'sense' you speak of. When we were forced to go to war against the dogs for the right to feed ourselves, I sensed when it was time to fight and when it was time to lay by and let other factors work for us, even though there were other rats, admittedly smarter than I, who disagreed."

I nodded. "I've heard it said that artists are often not the most intelligent of creatures, yet sometimes they have the ability to see through brick walls."

"So if poetry is not my 'medium,' as you say, what is? Warfare?"

"Many a warrior has been an artist, but I sense that circumstances have led you to miss your true calling. I believe, sire, that, in your heart of hearts, you're a painter."

It was as if I had spoken a magic word, for Cawdallor's eyes lit up.

"You know," he said, "back in my younger days, I used to frequent the parks and river banks where humans gathered with their paints and canvases. I spent many a happy hour watching them, marveling at how they could take brushes and daubs of color and re-create the scenes before them." Cawdallor stared at the empty wall above the sleeping diners. "A painter, eh?"

There was a faraway look in his eyes, yet when he managed to focus them upon me, he once again became all business.

"Ahem!" he said, clearing his throat. "An interesting idea, Teig." With a casual wave of his paw he added, "Well, perhaps I'll slap a little paint around–if I ever get the time."

His nonchalance didn't fool me, for there was still that glint in his eyes. More than a glint; I could practically feel the heat.

"There's an abandoned warehouse two up from the river on the Rue Chanteuse," I said. "I know for a fact it's chockfull of paint pots and every kind of brush. If Your Majesty wishes to try his paw at painting, you might start there."

"I'll think about it, Teig," he said, yawning. "Now, I believe I shall retire. You've provided me with stimulating conversation this evening, and in return, I wish to offer you your freedom."

"Your Majesty is most gracious," I said, bowing low.

Cawdallor wave his paw. "Nothing of the kind."

"Perhaps, sire, there will come a time when I can do something similar for you."

Cawdallor leaned forward and fixed me with his coal black eyes. "Not while we rats rule this land!"

Little changed in the days and weeks that followed. In the palace of Cawdallor the Rat King, the mice continued to serve up sumptuous dinners, the rats to glut themselves comatose, and the cockroaches to clean up the mess. I know because I had a spy: one of the waiters whose sister I was keeping for a snack should he fail to inform me of the goings on in Cawdallor's court.

Twylln, the head of the guards, did his best to provide nightly entertainments, though never again anything involving a cat. He did, however, bring in a goose, whose loud honking got a few laughs, but soon grew annoying. Dinner conversation was usually a spiritless debate about whether the head chef was losing his touch. Someone did mention seeing a few crude drawings on the walls in the nearby streets, but this remark drew little response.

Then one morning the rats woke to find a mural had been painted on the wall above their dining table. Though the execution left much to be desired, the theme appealed to the rats' simple tastes. It was the kind of heart-warming scene that a later illustrator would make famous in his nostalgic depiction of an American Thanksgiving feast, only instead of the viewer looking down the table past the balding uncles, cherubic aunts and glossy children to the grandparents, hovering over the roast turkey, the mural showed a contented family of rats about to tuck into a fresh human corpse.

Other paintings soon began to appear upon the walls that surrounded Cawdallor's palace. They were all quaint scenes depicting the glories of this Golden Age of Rats. Indeed, some speculated that these art works were proof that this *was* the Golden Age, for it is only in such times of peace and prosperity that the arts can flourish. The paintings seemed to spark an interest in the other arts. A few rats began to try their paws at playing music. The ukulele became popular, as did the banjo. Someone got up a chorus. Then a theatre opened up in the lake front district, followed by a water ballet gotten up by the river rats.

The only rats unhappy with these new developments were Twylln (who now found his nightly entertainments largely unattended) and, oddly enough, the king. It was noted the king looked much reduced. His hair had become dry and brittle. Bags under his eyes indicated a lack of sleep. Worst of all, he was losing weight, for instead of eating, Cawdallor sat playing with his food, making odd sculptures out of deep-fried fingers, separating out boiled eyeballs by color, cutting up grilled livers into whimsical shapes.

One morning, the rats awoke to find the mural in the banquet hall had been altered. Though it still depicted a feast, now there was something rather troubling about the appearance of the diners. There was a lean, hungry look in their eyes. The feeling of contentment had been replaced by a sense of tension and urgency. The painting hinted at an impending catastrophe, as if this just might be the diners' last meal.

Dining in the oppressed atmosphere created by this new painting, the rats found themselves eating more than ever. Squabbles broke out over the littlest of things: whose cup was whose; which table had more baskets of bread; why was there never enough catsup? Some rats began to take more interest in drinking than eating, while others chose to forego the table wines altogether in favor of the stronger spirits to be had in the dank watering holes down by the river.

Perhaps this need for stronger drink was in response to the paintings now popping up all over town, paintings that no longer depicted rats as plump, contented and affable, but sharp-toothed, sly and sinister. They more than hinted at the existence of a dark side in rats. A few rats declared these paintings a wake-up call, and called for a "moral renewal," but these fanatics were soon beaten down by cooler heads. Yet there was one thing all agreed upon: each new painting was more disturbing than the last, harsher in its depiction of rats and their way of life.

The general populace looked to Cawdallor to put an end to this mischief, to demand that the painter be found, and, at the very least, put somewhere he could no longer offend the sensibilities of good rats. The king, however, was no longer a decisive ruler, but a restless, nervous rat who ate little and sat scratching his claws on the arm of his throne and mumbling to himself. He seemed a rat possessed by either a demon or a great dream.

Perhaps it was the latter, for not only the rat kingdom, but the wider world seemed to be reaching the end of a long sleep. Everywhere men were awaking to new ideas, new directions, new dreams. Strange words entered their vocabulary: "epidemiology," "vector-borne infectious diseases," "*Yersinia pestis*," "population control." Suddenly, the killing of cats no longer seemed like such a good idea. In fact, cats were encouraged to reproduce and multiply. And as the cat population soared, the rat population plummeted. Cawdallor's subjects fared better than most, for his soldiers were fierce defenders of his kingdom. In well-organized counter-attacks, they drove back the cats and maintained control of food sources. But the cats learned from the discipline of the rats. A great cat general appeared and began to train his soldiers. His successes were immediate. Rat supply lines were cut, weapon caches destroyed, strategic positions overrun. It wasn't long before no rat was safe outside the palace walls, and when that happened, the rats were forced to go on rations, and in time, the rats began to take on the lean, hungry look of the figures in the mural on the wall in the banquet hall. It took Twllyn's heavy hand to maintain order. As for Cawdallor, the great Rat King had locked himself away in his private chamber.

"Your Majesty!" Twylln shouted, as he rapped upon the chamber door. "Your Majesty!"

"Go away!" cried the Rat King from within.

Twylln rapped harder. "Your Majesty, I really must speak with you. It's of the utmost importance."

The bolt was thrown back and the door opened just enough for Cawdallor to stick his head out. "What is it?"

Twllyn could hardly believe his eyes, so changed was Cawdallor. "Your Majesty, is that you?"

"No, it's Leonardo da Vinci. Now what do you want?"

"Sire, the cats have completely surrounded the palace. There is no way out. The last scraps of food were distributed days ago, and our subjects are starving, and many of our older, infirm citizens have begun to disappear."

"And what would you have me do?" Cawdallor said. "Look at me!" He pulled at the skin about his cheek. "Not enough meat to feed a mouse."

"Sire, the leader of the cats, who calls himself a general, wishes an audience with you. He says he's willing to offer a deal that will allow us to leave the city unharmed."

"Leave? Why leave?"

"Your Majesty, haven't you heard a word I've been saying? We're surrounded! We'll either end up eating each other, or being overrun by cats!"

"Oh, very well," Cawdallor said. "Tell this cat-general I can spare him five minutes. Where is he?"

"I am right here," I said, for I had been sitting in shadows and had heard everything.

"Teig!" Cawdallor exclaimed, breaking into a grin. "How many times I've thought of you, and now here you are!" Cawdallor sent Twylln away then opened the door wide to his chamber.

"Really, this is quite a surprise!" Cawdallor said, closing the door after I had passed through. "There's no one else on earth I would rather see than you just now." With a sweep of his paw, he directed my attention to the walls of his chamber. There wasn't a patch that didn't have a painting hanging on it, and dozens of canvases leaned against the stonework.

"I've seen you've done more than just 'slap a little paint around,'" I said.

"Yes, yes," said Cawdallor, rubbing his paws together. "So tell me, what do you think?"

I slowly walked about the room, examining each painting. There were still lifes and landscapes, portraits and illustrations. "Remarkable!" I exclaimed. "Quite remarkable!" But the best of the lot was a painting that sat upon the easel. Judging by the fresh paint, Cawdallor had been putting on the finishing touches. It was a scene of the guards in the great banquet hall hauling me forward by ropes about my neck. I leaned forward for a closer look.

"Of course, I still feel an amateur," Cawdallor said. "I'm only just now getting some command of color and forms."

"In no way would I call this amateurish," I said, straightening up. "Tell me, did I really look so abject?"

"I'm afraid you did, my friend. Yet believe me when I say I didn't paint this to humiliate you." Cawdallor ran a paw across his forehead. "You might say it's a study in the vagaries of life."

"Meaning, you rats have had the upper paw, and now we cats do."

"Yes, there's that, I guess," Cawdallor said, "but for me, the meaning is more personal. The day you were dragged into my hall was the greatest day of my life, for it was then I discovered who I truly am, not a king at all, but a painter." Sighing, Cawdallor took off the apron he had been wearing and hung it over the easel. "Only now I suppose

I must go back to being a king again. What is this offer of yours? I must warn you, you may have the palace surrounded, but we rats will not go down without a fight."

"I don't believe there's need for further conflict," I said. "I once told you I might someday do something for you. Well, that day has come. I'm prepared to offer you and your subjects safe passage out of the city. I'm afraid it's the best I can do. If my soldiers had their way, they'd attack this instant and make an end of it."

"So, when are we to leave?"

"Now!"

With cats lining both sides of the main road, Cawdallor led his subjects from the city and far out into the countryside. I was true to my word; no cat laid a claw on a single rat, but neither did we provide them with any provisions for the approaching winter. It was then that Cawdallor proved his greatness, for as the snows piled up, he seemed to be everywhere at once, cheering up the rats, giving them hope, finding food for them when all others had failed. Still, countless rats perished from cold and starvation, and it was many years before the rats were once again a prosperous community. By then, Cawdallor had worn himself out in service to his subjects. He never again painted a picture.

And upon the throne where Cawdallor the Rat King once sat, I now look out over the great banquet hall where merry cats feast. The mural above the dining tables has been left just as it was, for the irony of the changed situation is a great source of amusement to us. And next to the throne hangs the painting of myself, being dragged forward into the banquet hall by rats. I've put it there to remind us all of "the vagaries of life," as Cawdallor put it. Yet late at night, when the great hall is empty, I like to come here and just sit and study the painting, for there is within it evidence of greatness. It was the first masterpiece of a painter who had the misfortune to be a king.

· Michael ·

"Jesus, Serena!" Michael exclaimed. "You dreamed my dream!"

"*Your* dream?" Serena said, smiling.

"Yeah, an artist's dream."

"I see. So, the fact that I'm a weaver means I'm not an artist?"

"That's not what I meant."

Serena nudged Michael with her foot. "I think that's exactly what you meant, but we weavers are used to being slighted, so I'll let it pass."

"No, Serena, what I meant is that I also had an artist's dream."

"Do you want to tell me about it?"

"Later. Right now, I want to discuss your dream because it really spoke for me. It said what I couldn't seem to say earlier when I was trying to defend my choice of career."

"Michael, I wasn't attacking you for being a singer. I told you that you sing beautifully."

"Well, maybe it's just me, but all your talk about 'goodness over getting-ness,' and about how bad things are in the world, made me feel guilty for being someone who just wants to sing. I mean, it's obvious I'm not out there feeding the poor or trying to put an end to war."

"I'm not doing those things either."

"Yeah, but are those things really what's most important? I think your dream says they're not."

Serena shook her head. "I don't see that at all. Cawdallor gave up his painting in order that he might save his subjects."

"Okay, so where's the tragedy? I mean, you gave your dream a title: *The Tragedy of Cawdallor, the Rat King*."

"All right, on a personal level, it was a tragedy, but overall, it wasn't, unless you're talking about those cats being burned at the stake and all those people dying of the plague."

Michael waved his hand. "Forget the plague; the dream is not about the plague. It's about Cawdallor and the tragedy of the world losing a master painter."

"No, the tragedy would've been if he'd *not* given up his painting and gone on and played the fiddle while Rome burned."

"He was a painter, not a musician."

"You know what I mean."

"Yeah, but do you know what I mean?"

"I think I do. You're telling me one rat's ambition is more important than the greater good? A Mona Lisa is more important than the life of others?"

Michael shook his head. "Don't do that, Serena. I hate it when people put everything in terms of absolutes: 'Should I sing, or should I let starving children die?' 'Should I use the money I've saved to buy a new piano or should I put it towards my mother's kidney transplant?' If you tip the scales like that, well then, sure, the choice is obvious. Although..." Michael tapped his chest. "You know, there's something inside here that rebels at even those obvious choices, something that says, 'screw the starving kids, I'm gonna paint'!"

Serena tapped her own chest. "And something in here rebels against the artist who thinks his art is more important than people."

"But that's because you're still thinking in terms of absolutes. Most choices aren't like that. Maybe it's because we live in a day and age where we have more freedom, but, whatever the reason, we have more choices, and the artist, if he's any kind of an artist at all, must choose to follow his own heart."

"And what if the artist has only evil in his heart, because I can think of quite a few artists who the world would have been better off without?"

Michael grinned. "I know you're going to bombard me with caramels for saying this, but yeah, even if the artist only has evil in his heart, because art is like Pandora's Box, you open it up and out comes both good and evil. But I truly believe the world is enriched by art, in fact, I know it is, and sometimes the price the world has to pay is to put up with a few evil geniuses."

Serena said nothing, just tightened her lips and wrinkled her forehead.

"Serena, I'm going to use that disapproving look of yours to go back to a phrase you used earlier: 'the greater good.' I can't say that's something I put much store in."

"But how can you say that? You wouldn't be here if it wasn't for the fact of people putting the greater good above their own self-interest."

"Give me an example."

"Okay, how about the doctor who delivered you? He dedicated years and years of his life in study so you would have the greatest possible chance of survival."

"So, we should all be doctors then?"

"No, Michael, we each have our own unique way we can serve."

"That's right!" Michael exclaimed, jabbing the air with his finger. "That's right! We all have our own unique way we can serve, and the best way an artist can serve is to be an artist, not a king, and certainly not the savior of his people. Let the person whose talent it is to be a savior, be the savior, and let the artist be the artist."

"But it doesn't work that way! Sometimes a person has to do what he's called on to do, even when he doesn't want to do it."

"Even if he's unsuitable for the job?"

"Yes."

"You know, there's something that really stinks about that. There's something so life denying. Look at the people who've made a difference in this world. They didn't start out by saying, 'I'm going to dedicate my life to doing good.'"

Serena questioned with raised eyebrows.

"Okay, well, maybe a few of them did. But most just went about trying to live their lives. They found something they liked, something they were good at, something they had a talent for, and they stuck with it. And out of that came great works, out of that came art that changed people's lives, that made the world a better place, for here's the thing about art: it's far greater than the artist. The artist is human. The artist has his faults just like everyone else. In fact, you look at the artist and you say, how on earth did that awful person create works of such sublimity? Beethoven is a good example. They called him a beast, but where would the world be without Beethoven? Where would we be without the 'Pathetique' and the 'Appasionata,' without the nine symphonies? I'd rather have the music of Beethoven than save all the little rats of this world, for when the years go by, and the people have died, what endures, what do we remember? The people who are gone, or the works that continue to live and enrich our lives?"

"You forget, Michael, that each person's life is important to him. Would you, personally, trade your life for Beethoven's music? Yes, the loss of Beethoven's music would be a great tragedy. But a person's untimely death is also tragedy, if only to that person."

"I know that, Serena. But the point I'm trying to make is about the way people make a difference in this world." Michael leaned forward. "The people I've always admired are those who have been true to themselves, because, as you said, each person is unique, and if a person doesn't express himself out of that uniqueness, then his special gift will be lost, for no one else can duplicate it. You know what I think is the real tragedy? There are millions and billions of people out there who will likely never find out what their special talents are, who'll never get a chance to share their uniqueness. And there's something else I've noticed: not only is a person happiest when he knows who is, and can express it, he's of more benefit to the world. Take Marshall Banks. I admit he's not exactly a great humanitarian, but he brings such passion to his music, for the man was born to be a choral conductor. And what's the result? He not only inspires people like me, but he brings great beauty into the world, for there is no one, or nearly no one, who can interpret choral music the way he does. Tell me, Serena, what good would it be to save the world if there was no beauty in the world to save? What is the world for, or maybe I should ask, what are we for? To wreck our lives in saving others, or to be who we truly are in our heart of hearts? I'm not talking about someone acting out of selfishness, out of pure ego gratification. I'm talking about a person responding to what makes him tick, what gives him joy, because whatever that is, it will likely bring joy to others, and I think that is better than thinking you have to go out and save the world. Hell, Serena, that *is* saving the world."

Serena took in a big breath then slowly released it. "I don't know what to say to you, Michael. You speak with great passion. I only know that matters are often a lot more complicated than that."

"I know that, too, Serena. I'm not a fool even if I am an artist." He laughed. "What was it Teig said, the artist is someone who's 'not the most intelligent of creatures?'"

"You seem quite intelligent to me."

"Thank you. Now, I know it's late–"

"Early you mean. It's way past midnight."

Michael smiled. "Okay, early, but could I tell you *my* artist's dream, because I really don't quite know what to make of it?"

"Okay, just let me get more comfortable." Serena rearranged the pillows she had been leaning against. "Okay, go ahead."

Abbud and the Carnelian Cat

It is written that on Wednesday were the angels created from light. As is the case with light, angels neither sleep, eat nor drink. Neither do they tire, and they can endlessly sing praises to their maker. Having not free will, these great creatures are incapable of evil.

On Thursday were the jinn created from smokeless fire, and thus they cannot be seen. Like wisps of smoke, jinn can enter by way of the nostrils into the minds of other creatures. Unlike angels, jinn were granted free will, capable of good or evil. Yet upon their creation, jinn were deemed good, for nothing comes from Allah, the All Mighty Creator, that is not good.

Then on Friday, Allah created humans from clay, and they, too, were given free will. Being of clay, humans were not made invisible, as were the jinn, but given the special gift of form, and because of this, many jinn grew jealous.

"Why did we not deserve to be given form?" they said. "After all, is not fire greater than clay?"

Angry at Allah, many jinn rebelled by perpetrating foul deeds upon humans, and for this reason, Allah was forced to summon a great army of angels, and the angels did destroy all but a few jinn.

And this is where I come in; I who was given the name Hinn, meaning "little," because I am. Truth be told, I never saw the advantage of having form. I mean, who wants to slog over hill and dale when one can ride the wind unencumbered by flesh and bone? Besides, I've always had a soft spot for my earthbound brothers, so while other jinn were amusing themselves by whipping up tsunamis, firing up

The Dreams of Gerontius

volcanos and occasionally rearranging traffic signs during rush hour, I chose to sit on the sidelines, and thus was spared Allah's wrath.

When the angels finally got back to their usual job of singing praises, I chose to make amends for my fellow jinns' rambunctiousness by benefitting humans by means of dreams. Yet I cannot do this directly, but must have an intercessor, usually an animal. At first, I tried dogs, but dogs have very little influence on a person's dreams. The last thing someone wants when settling down for a good night's sleep is to have a malodorous dog breathing down his neck. Dogs are relegated to the foot of a bed for good reason.

Cats, on the other hand, are clean animals. The Prophet, peace be upon him, who was a great lover of cats and once cut off the sleeve of his robe upon which his cat Muezza was sleeping rather than disturb her, once knowingly drank water from a cup that a cat had previously drunk from. It is a known fact that a cat's purr shares many qualities with the rhythmic chanting that Sufis use to calm and heal. When a purring cat lies next to a man's head, the man is eased into a sleep devoid of all thoughts and inner disturbances. It is then that I can slip in through his nostrils and plant a dream.

Usually, I just try to give the sleeper something pleasant to dream about, though, upon occasion, this does not result in a favorable outcome for myself. One time I was providing a dream for a man who had a passion for delectable foods. I created for him a vision of a steaming plate of grilled fish seasoned with sumac and lemon. A platter of slow-cooked lamb, stuffed with rice, nuts and spices gave off an aroma that had him salivating on his pillow. But I must have put too much curry in his kibbeh, for my sleeping friend sneezed, and I was blown ass-wards back through his nasal cavity. Little as I am, it was not an experience I would care to repeat.

But sometimes I like to do something more than cause a slumbering gourmand to drool. It must be understood that we jinn were around for thousands of years before that Friday when Allah chose to create humans. In all that time, we became well aware of every source of magic, be it a spell that awakens a catatonic princess, or a formula which turns lead into gold. Furthermore, there is no treasure, no matter how cleverly secreted away, that we do not know of. Armed with this knowledge, I can offer a dreamer something that, if heeded, might provide a fortune for a beggar, or a possible escape for a trapped prisoner, or even turn those other dreams, the great waking dreams which drive a person to do what he does, into reality. There is, however, a caveat concerning these dreams: they always come with a proviso of one sort or another, and, being only the humble provider of dream, I cannot be held accountable for what a person does should he not heed the warning given.

Now, I have a small confession to make. Dream-making is more a sideline with me. My true passion is for travel, and being a jinn, I can travel fast, faster than a hawk swooping down upon his unsuspecting prey. It was while I was taking in the sights of Baghdad one day that I came upon Abbud, a poor carver. At first, I took no more notice of him than the countless beggars that haunt the Baghdad thoroughfares and tend to plug up traffic. Then I saw Abbud was selling something, so I swooped down to take a closer look. Abbud appeared half-starved, (a doumbek player could have played a tune on his ribcage). Yet despite this, he was sharing a bowl of watery fish soup with a stray cat. Surely, I thought, the Prophet, peace be upon him, would have been greatly pleased.

By why half-starved this carver, for he was young and seemed healthy in other respects? Surely such a man could have found work which would have afforded him a better diet. Then I turned my attention to a dirty cloth spread out on the ground upon which Abbud had arranged his carvings for the benefit of passersby to see and hopefully buy. The carvings, any one of which could have fit in the palm of one's hand, were all of cats. Yet, small as they were, these figurines were intricately carved, and each was in some way different despite many having similar poses. There were sleeping cats curled up with one paw wrapped around their noses. There were cats looking to pounce upon a mouse. There were cats licking one paw in preparations for a bath. There were even cats, sitting tall, sporting that imperious manner, which says, "You best hurry up and open the door for me!" Sadly, only a few people stopped to look at his wares. Most hurried past without a glance in his direction. It was obvious Abbud was in need of a good marketing agent.

At the end of a fruitless day, Abbud gathered up his carvings, and stumbled off in the direction of Baghdad's low rent district. Curious as to how and where this fellow cat lover lived, I followed along. The dwelling wherein he slept (to call it a hovel would have glorified it) was hardly big enough for him to stretch out in, and what little space remained was taken up by pieces of driftwood and stone, the makings for his carvings. A rat emerged from this pile of rubble, and Abbud pounced upon it, but the rat was quicker and escaped through a large gap beneath the door.

With a sigh, Abbud sat upon a torn reed mat and leaned his back against the wall. From the pocket of his baggy trousers, the only article of clothing he had to fend off the cold of the approaching night, he withdrew another small carving of a cat. Rather than being fashioned from ordinary sticks or stones, this one was made from a semi-precious stone, a blood-red carnelian, and had been polished so that even in the near darkness, it shone like a cut gem. For a while, Abbud just gazed at the carnelian cat before he began to rub it gently between his palms, as if by rubbing it he might bring forth a genie who would grant him three wishes, or at least tell him where a slower rat could be had. Then Abbud kissed the little carnelian cat before returning to his pocket.

Now I think I knew the answer to my earlier question as to why Abbud had not found a more profitable occupation. He loved his little carvings. It was the act of bringing these little cats to life that nourished his soul, and, for the time being at least, he appeared willing to forego nourishment of the flesh in pursuit of his art.

As Abbud he lay upon his side, his back to the door through which a chill breeze entered through the cracks, I thought of how I might benefit this poor artist and reviewed several old legends and a few incantations. While I was thinking, the stray cat squeezed in under the door, curled up beside Abbud and began to purr.

That was my cue. I slipped in and got to work. First, I had to deal with Abbud's troubled sleep, for even a cat's purr cannot completely soothe a body that is cold and hungry. In a dream, I placed Abbud before a large fire, and when I saw tiny beads of sweat forming upon his skin, I conjured up bread and cheese and a little wine, nothing too rich, for I did not want him to sleep too heavily. Then when he was sated and warm, I created for him a vision of himself dressed in silken robes of brilliant colors and adorned with jewels. I shod his feet in sequined slippers, and upon his head I placed a snow-white turban with one large emerald front and center. No prince, not even a king, was ever so splendidly adorned. Then from the fire I drew smoke and swirled it about until it was shaped into seven words:

A GREAT FORTUNE AWAITS YOU IN CAIRO.

The next day, Abbud took all his carvings to a pawnshop where he exchanged them for a few well-worn pieces of clothing. Then he hired on as a camel driver with a fat merchant whose trade goods were bound for Egypt. But before departing with the caravan, Abbud secretly buried his precious carnelian cat deep in the dirt within his dwelling where it would be safe.

I looked in on him and his fellow travelers from time to time as they made their perilous journey across the Arabian desert. Once they were nearly buried in a sandstorm; twice they were set upon by bandits; three times they came to wells that were dry. By the time the caravan reached Cairo, there were half as many camels and trade goods as when it started. The merchant, in an attempt to make up for some of his losses, tried to cheat Abbud by deducting from his pay the cost of the food Abbud had consumed along the journey. A shouting match ensued until finally Abbud, tired of arguing, accepted but half the pay due him. But as the merchant turned away, several gold coins fell from his purse, and Abbud snatched them up and disappeared before the merchant could do anything.

That night, after enjoying a sumptuous meal, Abbud slept in a comfortable bed for the first time in years. The next day, he set about finding the treasure that supposedly awaited him. This proved difficult. The problem was that the message he received in his dream was not specific. It did not state exactly *where* in the great city of Cairo he would find his great fortune. Abbud spent days, weeks, months searching in every inn, tavern, marketplace, street, and alleyway until he had but a few coins left. Finally, because he could not afford even the most miserable bed in the most disreputable inn, he was forced to sleep in the mosque. But while he was asleep upon the cold stone floor, robbers entered the mosque, intent on stealing any valuables they could find. The police, having been alerted to the possible theft, rushed into the mosque, but the robbers had already managed to escape. The police found the mosque empty save for Abbud, fast asleep. They yanked Abbud to his feet, accused him of theft and dragged the poor man off to jail, but not before beating him mercilessly and taking his last remaining coins.

The next morning, Abbud appeared before the seat of the local magistrate who demanded to know why Abbud, a thief, should not be punished by having one of his hands cut off. Abbud, his knees shaking, told the magistrate all about his dream and its message and his long journey from Baghdad and the months spent searching everywhere in Cairo for the treasure he was told awaited him, only to have his money run out and be forced to sleep in the Mosque.

Upon the conclusion of this story, the magistrate laughed so hard and for so long, his clerk feared his would have to summon a doctor.

"You fool!" the magistrate declared, once he could draw breath. "You came all this way because of a silly dream?"

Abbud, looking ashamed, hung his head and said nothing.

Gesturing toward the few hangers-on witnessing the courtroom proceedings, the magistrate said, "We've all had childish dreams about buried treasure and that sort of thing. Why, not long ago, I had a dream that if I were to dig in some poor man's hut, I would find a carving of some sort, which would bring me a great fortune, but only as long as I kept the carving in my possession. If I were to lose it, then all my wealth would disappear. Of course, it was all some make-believe nonsense I must have heard in some fairytale as a child."

The magistrate looked down at Abbud who now appeared quite excited. "Are you listening to me?"

Abbud's heart was pounding so hard, he could barely speak. "What did the carving look like?" he said.

"Don't tell me you're now going to go looking for it?"

"Please, sir," Abbud pleaded, "I must know."

"Oh, very well. It was a carving of a cat, colored red. About as big as my thumb. Much luck you'll have trying to find something that small." Yet the magistrate could tell that Abbud was taken with the idea. "Some people never learn," he muttered.

Then the magistrate, being a good man and realizing Abbud was a fool and not a robber, handed Abbud some money and sent him on his way. But Abbud knew himself to be no fool, for he had found the great treasure he sought. He now had only to return to Baghdad to claim it.

All told, Abbud spent nearly three years going and returning. Still, he found his tiny dwelling exactly as he left it. (As if anyone would have bothered with it.) He dug up the carnelian cat and rubbed the dirt off it then waited for good fortune to come his way. While waiting, he resumed his former occupation by displaying his cat carvings on the streets of Baghdad.

One day, a litter, bearing a princess, happened by. The princess had many cats, for she loved cats, and one in particular was her favorite. Seeing the little cat carvings, she ordered her servants to stop. Then she got out to examine Abbud's little cats. Impressed with the skill by which they were carved, she immediately offered Abbud a commission, to carve a life-sized figure of her favorite cat out of a piece of marble that she would supply. In addition, the princess told Abbud that she would not only provide him with a place to work, but also a dwelling, and servants to look after him.

Abbud was nearly beside himself with joy. (Actually, it was me beside him, back from a vacation at the Red Sea.) He made arrangements to start working the very next day. The cat, the princess' favorite, who was to be the subject of Abbud's carving, was gray in color with streaks of black. This presented a problem, for the marble the princess supplied was pure white. Abbud spent several days just observing the cat, studying his mannerisms: the way he walked, the positions he assumed when settling down for a nap, the way he behaved around the princess, the demands he made upon the servants.

The pose Abbud eventually chose to bring out of the marble was simply that of the cat sitting up, front legs straight, his tail wrapped around his feet. It was the details of the face wherein Abbud caught the cat's singular character, for the cat had a very wise and patient expression and his eyes often appeared to be peering right into the very soul of the viewer. It was these eyes which Abbud captured perfectly.

When the carving was finished, the princess was beside herself with joy. (Not me this time; I was touring the Seven Pillars of Wisdom.) The princess' friends were likewise enthralled, and soon Abbud was swamped with commissions. Abbud rented his own studio and hired several servants to keep the place clean while he worked. The demands for Abbud's carvings grew so great, rich people fought over the privilege of employing him.

Soon Abbud was a wealthy man, but a problem arose. Abbud was an artist, and most of those who commissioned him were not all that concerned with Abbud's talent for bringing out the true character of a cat. What they really wanted was a status symbol, something that would serve to flaunt their wealth. They wanted cats with emeralds for eyes, jeweled collars and silly little cat vests made with strings of pearls. The worst were those who insisted the cats be made of pure gold, which forced Abbud to learn metallurgy and mold making and the effects of certain fuels upon the production of fire. The work was very demanding, for melting gold is terribly hot work. (As if Baghdad wasn't hot enough already!)

One day while Abbud was working before a fiery kiln, he realized that, though he was now quite wealthy, he was not having much fun.

He remembered back to his first commission when, with just a few tools, a block of marble, and the skill of his hands, he succeeded in bringing out the true nature of the princess' favorite cat. Oh, how this this achievement had delighted him!

With a sigh, Abbud set aside the gold-filled crucible he had been holding over the fire, and from his pocket he took out the little carnelian cat. Since digging it up, he had never for a moment parted with it. The carnelian cat served to remind him of how far he had come since those days spent exhibiting his carvings on the streets of Baghdad. Though he was starving at the time, there was a certain excitement to his life, a feeling of possibilities, as if he were floating down a river, not knowing where he was going, but feeling both excited and fearful at the same time. But most of all, he felt free.

But the carnelian cat also reminded him of the pleasures of wealth and the gratification of being sought after, and also of the warning the Egyptian magistrate spoke of, that if the carnelian cat were ever lost, so too would be his good fortune.

Abbud sighed yet again. *What am I to do? Should I hold onto the carnelian cat and keep doing what I'm doing, making carvings which bring me wealth but no joy, or should I rid himself of the carnelian cat (which I love for its own sake) and thus relinquish my good fortune, but regain my freedom?*

Placing the carnelian cat between the palms of his hand, Abbud gently rubbed it back and forth, as if by doing so, the carnelian cat might give him an answer to his predicament.

My telling of the story of Abbud and the Carnelian Cat is now approaching its conclusion. It is not for me, Hinn, the little jinn, to provide an ending. Obviously, Abbud is faced with a dilemma, and he has to come to a decision. But, as with most predicaments, nothing is a simple as it seems. If it is believed that the conclusion to this story hinges upon a choice between fame and fortune, or artistic freedom, I would suggest that is only partially the case. Often answers are like treasures buried deep; one must dig for them.

So, I shall leave it to someone wiser than myself to decide what

Abbud should do. But that someone must take care lest he fail to give serious consideration to the story of Abbud and the Carnelian Cat! Otherwise I, Hinn, the little jinn, might one night slip in through his nostrils while he's sleeping. And wouldn't that be fun!

· Michael ·

"Now, don't tell me that dream wasn't inspired by Gerontius," Serena said.

"My dream was inspired by a cat, all right," Michael said, "but it wasn't Gerontius."

"Explain."

"Let me tell you a little story first. When I was a kid, I loved to go beachcombing. I'd get up at the crack of dawn to be down on the beach before anyone else. I always had a sense of anticipation, like maybe I'd find something really valuable that had washed up on the shore."

"And did you?" Serena said.

"Most of the time, if I were lucky, I'd maybe find a ball or perhaps a toy that wasn't too beat up. But there was this one time, right after a big storm at sea, when I found a lifeboat that must have come off a ship, only it wasn't exactly like your usual lifeboat. I called it my Persian Slipper because that's what it reminded me of. It had this really high stern, like the heel of a shoe, and the bow came to this sharp point that sort of curled back, like a Persian slipper you might see worn by a genie or a caliph in an illustration from *The Arabian Nights*.

"Anyway, it was a really cool boat, and I wanted it. The problem was it was stuck in the sand and it weighed a ton. After much stressing and straining, I managed to push it out into the water where it floated. My plan was to push it along the water's edge until I got nearer to home. But the Persian Slipper was so heavy, it wasn't long before I was totally exhausted. So, my next plan was to beach it, which I managed to do, then wait for one of my parents to come looking for me. I got in the boat and stretched out on the bottom. By this time, the sun was well up, and it was getting pretty hot. Tired and warmed by the sun, it wasn't long before I fell asleep.

"But here's the thing. When I woke up, the Persian Slipper was gone, and I was lying in the sand."

"You're kidding!" Serena exclaimed. "Did someone come along and claim it?"

Michael shook his head. "If someone had tried to take it, I would have surely woken up."

"So, did you just dream up the Persian Slipper?"

"To this day, I don't really know. I've always had an active imagination, and I must have been only six or seven when this happened, so maybe it was all just a dream. But there I was marooned on the shore, and that's went I saw this sticking out of the sand next to me."

From his pocket, Michael took a small red figure of a cat and held it out toward Serena.

Serena gasped. "Michael, it's the carnelian cat!" But before Serena could take the little figurine, Gerontius batted it out of Michael's hand.

"Gerontius!" Serena scolded. "What's gotten into you?"

Gerontius, his tail twitching, turned the figurine over with his paw.

"Why do you suppose he's so interested in it?" Serena said. "Because it's of a cat?"

"I think because of its smell, though I swear I washed it clean."

"Smell?" Serena said.

Michael sighed. "I'm not sure I should tell you this. It's kind of gross."

"Tell me anyway."

"Well, you know that dog I was talking about earlier, the one the lady on the first floor owns?"

"You mean Yum-Yum?"

"Right, well, about noon today, I was getting off the bus by the corner. I'd been over at the university, going over some last-minute things concerning the concert. Anyway, the bus had just started forward when out of the blue comes Yum-Yum chasing a cat."

Serena brought her hands to her face. "Oh, no!"

"I'm afraid so," Michael said. "I doubt the driver even knew what happened. Probably thought he'd run over a rock or something."

"Yum-Yum?" Serena said.

"The bus kind of squished him."

Serena covered her ears. "I don't want to hear any more."

"But wait! Here's the thing," Michael said, picking up the carnelian cat. "I've had this little cat since I the day I found it on the beach. I have a special place on my bookshelf where I always keep it. So here I am, just off the bus, looking down on poor Yum-Yum with his guts spilled all over the place, and what do I see?" Michael held up the figurine.

"It was inside of Yum-Yum?" Serena said.

"That's right."

"Are you sure it's the same figurine?"

"Of course, I'm sure. Besides, when I got back to my apartment, it wasn't on the shelf where I keep it."

"So how on earth did it get inside of Yum-Yum?"

Michael shook his head. "I haven't the faintest idea."

· Gerontius ·

Alas, poor Yum-Yum, I knew him not well enough to have gone messing about with his living arrangements. I thought I was giving him liberation, but, sadly, final liberation was the result.

Well, Yum-Yum, my not-so-great-conversationalist friend, may you find yourself not confined to a little yard in your next life. Perhaps you'll be reborn as a great bird, able to soar through the heavens in endless freedom. A turkey buzzard would be good. A buzzard is long-lived, and given your past eating habits, you'd likely relish a buzzard's cuisine.

As for the carnelian cat returning to Michael, it defies explanation. Chance cannot explain it; there are just too many variables involved. First, Marshall Banks cast his covetous eye upon Michael's treasure only to be foiled by my willingness to swallow it. Then I inadvertently passed it along to that little turd-eater, who, thanks to me, had learned to dig out from his backyard prison, only rather than using his new-found freedom productively, he abused it by chasing after cats, which sadly resulted in his being run over by a bus, the very one that Michael has just exited! No, chance cannot explain this. It is Fate playing her hand again. But what is she saying, Michael, other than that you are a very charmed person?

It seems to me that the carnelian cat found its way home to you, Michael, because it is your tutelary spirit, whose job demands that she look after you. That your tutelary spirit has taken the form of a cat is no coincidence, for cats are curious, creative and imaginative, qualities that you, Michael, as a musician, share. No wonder Marshall Banks wanted to take the carnelian cat from you. As a fellow musician, he likewise sensed its power. But keep in mind cats are also independent, valuing their freedom above all else. It is something to do with freedom which your carnelian cat has been trying to tell you through your dream. But before I say more, I want to hear what you and Serena have to say.

· Michael ·

"I remember I dreamt about Abbud and the carnelian cat the night after Gerontius bit Marshall Banks," Michael said. "I went to bed very upset, and didn't sleep well, which explains why so much of this dream just doesn't make sense."

"Any part in particular?" Serena said.

"For one, the part where Abbud has to go all the way to Egypt when the treasure was in Baghdad all along."

"I think that part *does* make sense. It's the idea of the hero's journey. Abbud just couldn't have the treasure given him on a silver platter; he had to earn it."

"You mean by going to Egypt and having the stuffing, to use a nicer word, beaten out of him."

"Yes, just as Ulysses had to spend ten years and go through all those perilous adventures before he could get back home; or in the Arthurian legend where Sir Perceval was forced to spend years in search of the Holy Grail just because he didn't ask the right question; or to use a more recent example, Dorothy having to bring the broomstick of the Wicked Witch of the West to Oz before she could get back home to Kansas."

Michael clicked his heels three times. "'There's no place like home. There's no place like home. There's no place like home.'"

"Exactly," Serena said.

"So what is the purpose of all that suffering?"

"To gain wisdom," Serena said. "It is not enough for Abbud to find the treasure; he must know how to use the treasure wisely."

"Okay, so, what great wisdom did Abbud gain?" Michael said.

"What you just said a second ago."

"What did I say?"

" 'There's no place like home.' "

"What, a shack where the cold wind blows in through the cracks in the door?"

Serena shook her head. "Home is a metaphor for introspection. Wisdom is not to be found by overt action, but by quietly seeking answers within."

Michael was silent for a while before saying, "I was afraid you'd say something like that."

"I didn't mean to trouble you."

"It's not that. It's just that, you've probably deduced, I'm not exactly an introspection kind of guy, but given all that has been going on with preparing for the concert and the thing with Marshall Banks, this weird dream gave me something like what you call a 'gut feeling.' "

"Care to share?"

"I'm not sure I can put the feeling into words."

"You might try to do what I do. I sit quietly and concentrate on the feeling and see what comes up."

Michael took a deep breath then closed his eyes.

"Just try to block out any extraneous thoughts and focus on the feeling," Serena said.

Michael's brow furrowed as he concentrated.

"It's important for you to try to relax."

Slowly the lines in Michael's forehead relaxed, and he was quiet for a long time, so long that, after five minutes, Serena began to wonder if he had fallen asleep.

"Michael?" Serena whispered.

Michael opened his eyes. When he spoke, it was in a quiet voice. "Remember me saying I hate any arguments framed in absolutes, like having to choose between buying a new piano or paying for my mom's kidney transplant?"

Serena nodded.

"Well, it seems that's exactly what my dream is doing. It's saying that Abbud, if he wishes to regain his artistic freedom, must give up success and return to a life on the streets. As if there wasn't some other alternative."

"Such as?"

"Such as continuing to be a successful carver, only choosing to be more selective about what sort of commissions he takes."

"The Buddhists would say that's 'taking the middle way,'" Serena said.

"Exactly."

"Okay, so how does all this relate to you?"

"Because, if I'm interpreting my gut feeling correctly, the dream is suggesting that I might want to give up my singing career."

"I see," Serena said. "Just out of curiosity, what would that feel like, giving up your singing career?"

"It would feel like death."

"Good death, or bad death?"

"What?"

"Unless something dies, something else, perhaps something greater, cannot be reborn."

"Lovely," Michael said as he rubbed his forehead.

"Maybe I shouldn't say anything more," Serena said. "At least until you've given yourself more time to think about your dream."

"No, Serena, I'd like to hear what you have to say. Maybe it will help me figure out what I've been feeling."

"Let me first say that I can't imagine what it would be like to give up something you worked so hard on. I've never invested time in anything the way you have in your singing career."

"You're equivocating," Michael said.

Serena smiled. "I admit to being a bit of a coward. I just don't want to say something that's maybe all wrong and will only add to your frustration."

"Say it anyway. I can take it, I think."

"Well then, perhaps your dream is telling you that you *should* give up your career singing, or at least rethink it. Or more accurately, I think it's telling you that your singing career may not be serving you anymore."

"So, what are you suggesting, that I should sell my piano and take a job selling life insurance?"

"No, you should take your time and think about what it is that brings you joy. I think that is basically what your dream is saying. Abbud found that his success did not bring him joy. That's often the way it is with people who have worked hard to achieve something."

"Which explains the high suicide rate among doctors."

"Something like that."

"This is a little off the subject, though not really. Did you ever hear someone say they'd love to be able to play the piano?"

Serena nodded.

"What they mean is they don't want to sit at the piano, practicing day after day, month after month, year after year. They just want to sit down at the piano and start playing. Imagine how fun that would be! It would be like being able to fly by just spreading out your arms. But in reality, I know piano players who spend weeks and months in order to master just one really difficult piano piece, and in the end, they find that all that slaving away over the keyboard has sucked all the joy out of playing.

"You know, I start singing when I was just a kid. I was chosen to be a chorister in the university choir because I had this sweet soprano voice and could sing on pitch. Of course, I didn't know a thing about music. It was all new to me, but it was all fun. And when the whole choir sang, boys and men together, especially when we were performing in the university chapel with its great acoustics, the sound sent chills up my spine. More than that, actually, it was like I was being lifted up to the vaulted ceiling.

"You know, Serena, I don't think the dream is telling me to give up singing at all; I think it's telling me to recapture that feeling I had when I was a boy who knew zilch about singing, but was soaring to the heavens."

· Gerontius ·

The exercise you had Michael perform, Serena, reminds me of an experience my friend Julia once had. Julia, of course, was the cat Sigmund Freud had the pleasure of having as a house-mate. Julia spent a lot of time observing Freud working with his patients, sometimes to her detriment. Like you, Serena, Freud knew that relaxation was the gateway to the inner realm. He would use his pocket watch to induce a state of deep relaxation in his patients by having them focus upon his watch as he swung it back and forth by its chain. Julia was mesmerized by this and would often follow this pendulum motion until she entered into a state of deep hypnosis, which sometimes lasted for hours. Once she was convinced she was a dog, and only came to her senses when Mrs. Freud, exasperated by Julia's repeated attempts to bark, poured half a bottle of hairball medicine down Julia's throat.

That aside, let me say, Michael, that your success in getting to the source of your gut feeling makes me feel that my time spent with you has been well rewarded. When I reflect upon some of my other relationship with humans, I realize that has not always been the case. Perhaps I should not be too hard on myself. Such success usually requires time and experience. You humans are blessed with long lives. You have time to learn, to grow, to discover that which gives you pleasure, to glean knowledge from that which causes suffering, and, hopefully, before the sands of time run out, come to possess one of the life's greatest rewards: wisdom, and perhaps also a little time to pass that gift on to someone else.

Within the short lifespan of a cat, all that represents a pretty steep learning curve, which is why I consider my many lives more as one life lived in many stages. My first life, which in some ways was my most pleasurable, makes me think about what you just said, Michael, about being a chorister. Like you, I had so much to learn! How to procure a meal; how to avoid *being* a meal (and, as a consequence, how to get down out of a tree). And because cats have been tasked with benefiting mankind, I had to learn the art of accommodation, which entailed learning the human language and, if such a thing is possible, getting a sense of how the human mind works. Yet despite my inexperience, each day of my first life brought another revelation, a new adventure, an unexpected joy.

I'm uncertain about how much wisdom I gained during some of my later lives, especially my caternity days spent with my fellow nighttime revelers. Yet even debauchery grants a few lessons, or as Pliny the Elder said, "In vino veritas." I would say the same thing about soused herring.

Yet having reached the final stage upon which all players must tread, I can say with confidence that whichever of my many lives I look back upon, my greatest source of wisdom came not from any experience or act of doing or spoken word, but from dreams. Humans speak of the "web of life," how all things are intricately interconnected. What they often fail to realize is that this interconnectedness does not end with the physical. Woven into this wondrous web are stories, myths, legends and especially dreams, all of which are as vital and as real and as necessary as shared DNA. The role of cats in this mysterious union is, as Hinn, the little jinn, so knowingly pointed out: as intercessors, the ones charged with joining the sleeping brain of humans with the rich treasure-trove of all collective wisdom. It is our gift to mankind. Which explains why a man is incomplete without a cat!

And that reminds me of something I must do before the sun brings a new day.

· Michael ·

"Look, Serena, Gerry-cat must be feeling much better!" Michael said this in response to Gerontius just having jumped out of the open window. "Maybe I won't need to take him to the vet after all." He turned to look at Serena. "Serena?"

"Hmm? Sorry, I must have drifted off."

"I'm not surprised. It can't be that much longer before the sun comes up." Michael swung his legs out over the edge of the window seat and began to put on his shoes, which he had taken off earlier.

"You know, considering how this night began, with me all upset because I couldn't find Gerry-cat after having kicked him, I must say this has been quite an extraordinary night."

Serena, looking sleepy-eyed, pushed herself up until she was leaning back against the wall. "Extraordinary?"

"I mean, how often does a person get to explore dreams and their meanings with someone and to talk about really important things?"

Serena smiled. "Not very often," she said.

Michael turned to look at Serena. "You know, with all that's been happening with me—the concert and being snubbed by Marshall Banks and losing my chance to sing in Carnegie Hall—I've been pretty much at my wit's end. But now, having been able to share things with you, I don't feel so bad. In fact, I don't think I even care anymore about the Carnegie Hall gig."

"I hope I've been of help. Oh, by the way, it has been a good night for me as well."

Michael looked a little chagrinned. "Sorry. I know I must sound like a pretty self-absorbed guy, but I want you to know that I really enjoyed hearing what you had to say because you're someone who's really thoughtful, and in my line of work, I don't always come across someone like that. I mean, if you look in the dictionary under 'self-absorbed,' you'll find 'musician' mentioned."

"I don't think you're all that self-absorbed, Michael. Not any more than me anyway."

"Really? Because now that I've gotten to know you, Serena, I really like you a lot, and I'm hoping you might like me as well," Michael hung his head. "Jesus, I'm sounding like some lovelorn adolescent."

Serena placed her hand upon Michael's "It's no crime to tell someone you like them, Michael, especially if that someone likes you as well."

Michael smiled. "In that case, what would you say that after we've both gotten a little shuteye, we do something together later on? Maybe go for a walk or out to dinner where we discuss some Cassian over a glass of wine."

Serena looked thoughtful. "I'd prefer we discussed Origen."

Michael stared at Serena, wondering whether she realized he'd been joking about Cassian.

Serena patted Michael's hand. "I'm just kidding. I'd love to share a glass of wine if for no other reason than just to be with you, Michael."

Michael stood up. "In that case, I better go and let you get some sleep."

But as Michael turned, Serena, reached out and took his hand. "Michael would you just…just lie here beside me?"

"You mean…"

"No, I mean just for us to lie next to each other and go to sleep."

Michael smiled. "Sort of like brother and sister?"

"Actually, I was thinking more of Tristan and Isolde the Blonde."

Michael lay next to Serena. "You're talking about the opera?"

Serena snuggled up against Michael. "Let's discuss it later."

· Gerontius ·

Phew! I made it back, and carrying a load, no less. God grant that if I should ever get another life, I spend it with someone whose apartment is on the ground floor.

Mew!

No, I'm not talking to you, little one.

Mew! Mew!

Not so loud! Can't you see Michael and Serena are sleeping? No, don't–oh, very well, walk all over Michael then. He sleeps like the dead anyway. Actually, the dead don't sleep all that well.

Mew! Mew!

Now, don't go wandering off like that. You're about to fall off the window seat.

Mew! Mew!

Yes, and it's a long way for a little kitten to fall. Here, let me move you back on top of Michael.

Mew! Mew!

Why are you wandering off again! Can't you stay put? Let me give you a little bath. Perhaps that will settle you. Ugh! You taste like dirt. We'll, it's no wonder, seeing you've been living under that garden shed. I had the devil of a time getting you out, you know.

Mew! Mew!

What are you trying to tell me, little one? Are you hurt? Here, let me look you over. Hmm, no, you look all right. But wait! What is the matter with your eyes? You can't see, can you? Oh, my little friend, you're blind!

Mew!

If only I had known I would have gotten you out from under that shed a long time ago. At least I had the sense to bring you the occasional mouse.

Mew!

Hush now, you're here, and Serena, who is very kind, will take care of you. Actually, I think both Serena *and* Michael will be looking after you, for I suspect they will soon be moving in together.

Mew!

Yes. Now what's that you've found on Michael's shirt? Oh, it's where that glutton spilled some pancake syrup. Yes, go right ahead and lick it. It's not much in the way of food, more like the dream of food, but at least it's something.

My, you have a nice purr! A real Sufi's chant! That tells me I can expect great things from you, little one. The tragedy of your blindness will only serve to make you a more thoughtful and introspective cat, capable of continuing the work I've only just started here with Michael and Serena. Of course, you'll first need to study your new housemates, to learn their language, to learn the strange way they think. Then once you get to know them, you must guide them.

Mew?

How? Through dreams, of course. Each night you must rest your head between Michael and Serena's and soothe their fevered brains with your purring. Then once you've settled them deep beneath Oblivion's waters, wrap and swathe them round in dreams, for it is in dreaming that we awaken.

Now, go to sleep, little one. Curl up there on Michael's soft tummy. Let him wake with a few flea bites. And while you sleep, I'll make my way to the rooftop, for I dearly want to see one more sunrise before I depart from this my ninth, and final, life. I do hope my friend Walter will be up on the rooftop to share the sunrise with me. What would be better than to be wafted up from this world on a cloud of cigarette smoke?

So, farewell, Michael and Serena. I leave you the care of my little blind friend along with my blessings. And this, too: a final dream.

The Tin Merchant's Nephew

"Now, I'll not be having you bullying this boy that's coming with him, do you hear?"

To Father's command, my brother grinned like the devil he was.

Father cuffed Myghal hard alongside the head, which only made him grin the more. "I mean it, now. This sale is too important, and I'll not have you spoiling it. Save your fists for Jacka Moyle and his bunch."

"Taking to boot kissing them dark foreigners, have you Da?" Myghal said.

This time Father hit Myghal so hard he slammed up against the far wall. It still didn't wipe the grin off his face. Myghal got up, spat blood, then made for the door. But as he passed Father he said, "Oh, I forgot, them foreigners don't wear boots."

Father swung around to give Myghal a kick, but Myghal was already out the door. Father turned to me. "You'll watch him, won't you Steren? I hear the boy is the merchant's nephew. He won't take kindly to our Myghal knocking his nephew senseless."

"Yes, Father, I'll watch him, but watching is about all I can do. You know Myghal; you know how he likes to fight."

Father nodded, looking worried.

"Much like his father," I added.

Father grinned, the same devilish grin as Myghal's. "But I know when it's time to fight and when it's time to do business. Myghal doesn't."

"Then send him to work with Uncle Jory this morning. Let him take Cador. You know how Myghal likes to ride that horse."

Father placed his hand upon my shoulder. "You've a good head on your shoulders, Steren. I said it before and I'll say it again, it's too bad you weren't born a man. As it is…"

He need not finish his sentence, for we both know it's conclusion: as it is, Myghal will one day inherit the tin mine, to do with as he pleases.

"Don't worry about Myghal," I said. "He may be quick tempered, but he knows how to get others to do his bidding."

"That he does," Father said, holding up his big fist. "With this!" We laughed and were still laughing when Talek, one of the other mine owners, stuck his head in through the open door.

"They're just now coming ashore, Kenwyn."

I followed along as Father and Talek went to the water's edge. A large row boat was being pulled ashore by two barefooted blacks whose muscles rippled as they dragged the boat over the gravel. It was not the first time I'd seen men of such color, but it had been a while since they had come to our shores, which made the sale of my father's tin all the more important.

Sitting athwart the boat was a heavily bearded man whose skin, though dark, was much lighter than that of the two hauling in the boat. He waited until the boat was firmly aground before gathering up his loose garment, like the robes of our Druid priests, and stepping over the gunwale. Myghal was right, the foreigners wore no boots, but leather soles bound over with strapping across their feet. It wasn't until the man was out of the boat that I saw the other passenger, a boy as thin as the man was broad. He slung one leg up over the gunwale then quickly yanked it back, exclaiming as he did so.

Talek, who knew a bit of their language, grinned. "The boy says the water's cold." We all laughed, and I wondered what manner of place the boy must come from where the sea was not cold. Or maybe the boy was touched. I bit my lip in worry, for Myghal was a terror to those who were weak.

Yet on closer inspection, the boy seemed right enough, for a foreigner at any rate. I suppose one of his own kind might have even judged him handsome. To me he looked soft, incapable of a day's work in the mines. That said, I was drawn to his eyes as he stared in wonder upon our green hills. I remembered what Father said of the land these foreigners came from, that it lay far away across a great bottled up sea, where there were few trees and vast stretches of sand, looking like a pale ocean frozen up. I could not fathom such a place, and suspected that were I to see it, likely I would have the same look as this boy, seeing our good green land for the first time.

There were exchanges made between Father and the man from the boat, awkward greetings and introductions. Then Father turned to me. "Take charge of the boy, Steren. Show him around, make him welcome."

Either the boy was smarter than I thought, or he knew some of our words, for he immediately came up to me. He made a bow and spoke what I took as a greeting.

Returning his bow felt awkward, for it is not our custom. "Dynnargh dhis," I said, which is the way we Cornish say, "Welcome."

When I straightened up, the boy was smiling and pointing to my red hair. Then he said something to his uncle and laughed. I hid my irritation behind a smile. "Would you like to see some of our animals?" I said.

Not understanding, he shook his head, so I pointed to the shed, and set off in that direction. As he followed along behind, I felt his eyes still on my hair. I swung back the shed door and was met with a smell I've always loved: the warm, earthy odor of animals.

"That's Cador, our horse," I said, pointing. "Don't get too close, for he is as fierce as the king he was named for."

I should have used gestures to make my meaning clear. Before I could stop him, the boy, marched right up to Cador and started scratching just above his muzzle. I had seen Cador nearly take a man's hand off for doing the same. Yet Cador not only tolerated the boy's touch, but appeared to take pleasure from it. The boy started crooning to him. I say crooning, for it was not true singing, the tune being terribly off pitch. Yet there was something soothing about it. Cador was affected, too, and placed his great cheek alongside the boy's.

"Do all foreigners have such a way with animals?" I said.

He did not answer, but continued his strange lullaby. I waited, hoping Myghal would not come along, for he thought of Cador as his horse, and I feared what he would do, seeing the affection Cador was showing the boy.

"There are more animals I can show you," I said. I pointed to Tamsyn and her kitten, lying atop a pile of straw. The boy hurried past me to pet the kitten even as Tamsyn was giving it a bath. Tamsyn yawned then rested her head upon her forepaws.

"There were six kittens," I said, "but Father drowned them. He usually drowns them all, but this time he let me keep this one, as this may be Tamsyn's last litter."

The boy spoke a question. I shook my head, not understanding. He brought his hands together in the shape of a bowl. "Yes, of course," I said, and lifted the kitten by the scruff of her neck to place in his hands. The kitten protested, and her mewing made the boy laugh. "Do you not have cats where you come from?" I said.

He lifted up a section of the kitten's hair, implying it was different. He did the same thing with her ears. The kitten, not liking her ear pulled, batted him with a paw. The boy cooed an apology, which the kitten must have accepted, for she climbed to his shoulder where she sat, purring into his ear.

What a strange fellow you are, I thought, to be so affectionate with dumb beasts. I could not picture Myghal showing such tenderness. The only pleasure Myghal got from kittens was when Father gave him the job of drowning them.

As I was thinking this, the devil himself strolled into the shed. Though Myghal acted for all the world as if we didn't exist, he was whistling, which was always a bad sign. I tugged on the boy's sleeve. "Let me show you the pigs. They're out back."

The boy said something that again I did not understand. This gave Myghal the opportunity he likely had been looking for. He mocked the boy, repeating back his own speech, only garbling it up. The boy took no offense, but turned toward Myghal and smiled. Myghal strode over, stopping just short of the boy, who bowed slightly and gave Myghal the same greeting he had given me earlier.

Now, I confess Myghal is a good actor, and funny when he's a mind to be. He bowed in turn, feigning welcome, though his words were anything but. "All you foreigners eat your own shit," he said with a friendly grin. "That's what makes you so black."

"Myghal!"

Myghal bowed again. "Why don't you screw my sister since you don't have yours here to screw."

I struck Myghal as hard as I could, but it was like straw striking rock; I doubt he even felt it. The boy now knew somewhat was wrong. He looked to me with questioning eyes. I tried to reassure him. "My brother has his way of joking about people, but he doesn't mean anything by it."

To this, Myghal hawked and spat at the boy's feet. Then he moved even closer to the boy until they were nearly touching. I was surprised the boy did not shrink away, for he was not half Myghal's size. Yet neither did he rise to the challenge. His look was one of resignation coupled with a touch of sadness, but no trace of fear.

Myghal saw this, too, and it must have galled, for Myghal fed on others' fear. I saw Myghal clench his fist, and I moved to put myself between him and the boy, but Myghal swept me aside with a stiff arm, and I fell hard upon my tailbone.

"Myghal," I said, tears running down my face, "remember what Father said. If you hurt this boy, if you spoil the sale, Father will kill you."

I thought Myghal was going to strike the boy, but instead he grabbed the kitten still sitting upon the boy's shoulder. Then he tightened his fist. The kitten's pitiful cry was cut off by the crunch of her bones breaking.

"Oh, Myghal!" I said, sobbing. "How could you?"

Myghal opened his fist. The poor little kitten lay quiet in his hand, a little blood dribbling out of her mouth. Laughing, Myghal dropped the dead kitten at the boy's feet. He was still laughing as he led Cador out of the shed.

I crawled over the dirt floor and took up the kitten. To her blood dripping upon my skirt, I added the water of my tears. I cried not only for the loss of the kitten, but also out of fear of what might come of Myghal's cruelty. What would this boy tell his uncle? Likely that we are all savages, and they should have no dealings with us.

The boy had been a long time silent. I looked up to find him looking at me, yet not looking, for he seemed to be going over something in his mind. Then he knelt down and reached to take the kitten from me. I pulled back, not wanting him bloodying his clothes as I had done. The boy placed his hands over mine. Then with surprisingly strong fingers, he pried mine away from around the kitten.

"Don't!" I cried. "There's nothing to be done. She's dead, and if you handle her, you'll ruin your clothes."

I think he actually understood, but that didn't stop him from taking the kitten anyway. He said something. I shook my head. He repeated his words and pointed to the kitten then wiggled two of his fingers as if they were little legs running over the ground.

"I don't understand!"

He placed the kitten in my hands, then repeated the gesture again, this time using both hands so there were four little legs running.

I thought him daft. "She can't run; she's dead."

"Dead," he repeated.

I poked the kitten with my finger. "Yes, dead. Myghal killed her." My tears, which had stopped, began to flow again. "I wish it were not so."

He nodded, looking at me with a sadness to match my own. Then he began to move one of his hands in slow circles above the kitten. I watched awhile before it came to me what he was going to do. Moreover, I knew he could do it, though I didn't know how I knew. There had been times when I sensed a thing was going to happen even before it did. I had that same feeling now, only much stronger.

"You're going to bring her back to life, aren't you?"

He said nothing, but continued passing his hand over the kitten. I wanted him to perform this miracle, not only that I might have my kitten alive once more, but also that I might see this thing happen and know the wonder of it. But what would be the result? Young as I was, I knew the world is not changed by miracles small or large, and Myghal, who hated all good that did not benefit himself, would not be pleased to discover his strength had failed against a helpless kitten.

With one hand, I reached out and stopped the boy's hand. "Don't," I said, "I know you are trying to do good, but I couldn't bear to think of Myghal killing the kitten a second time. As it is, she suffers no more."

He nodded and actually appeared grateful for my stopping him. He began to gather stalks of straw and to plait them together. I helped and together we wove a burial basket for the kitten. I then covered her with the kerchief I kept in my pocket.

"Come," I said, taking up the basket. I led him down to the water's edge then pointed to the great granite mount that rose up just offshore. "That's where we'll bury the kitten, out there upon the Mount. That's what we call it, though its real name is Carrack Looz en Cooz, the Gray Rock in the Woods."

He looked about for a boat to take us there.

"We'll walk," I said, wiggling two fingers.

His eyes went wide, and I laughed.

"The water looks deep," I said, "but the tide's out." I took off my boots and stepped out into the water, which barely came up over my ankles.

He stood staring at our watery pathway. I thought him afraid and took hold of his hand. But what I thought was fear, was just his thoughtful way of looking at the world. I waited as he stood, taking it all in: the grey skies mirrored in the standing water, looking for all the world like a vast sheet of hammered tin; and the Mount rising up out of the steely waters like a dream castle all in green. For me to say it this way meant I was seeing it through his eyes, all fresh and new. To the boy, used to softer climes, our Cornwall must have appeared a proud and haughty queen, yet she is all the more beautiful for her coldness.

Taking his hand from mine, he ran on ahead.

"Watch for the sinking sands!" I warned, pointing to a circle of sand different in color. Then I feigned being sucked down. He nodded then ran on ahead. Halfway to the Mount, he stopped and spun about, his loose sleeves billowing out like sails. It made me laugh to see his pleasure.

We reached the Mount, and I led him to a fresh water spring high up the steep slope, one that is hard to find unless one knows where to look. Water comes bubbling out of the rocks and tumbles down into a mossy catch basin overhung by the exposed roots of a giant of the woods. To me, this spring with its pool of clear, cold water is as sacred as any of those rings of stones standing out upon the headlands. As a child, I imagined it the home of the piskies, who on moonlit nights could be seen dancing about, should anyone prove brave enough to spy on them.

"I think we should bury the kitten here," I said, pointing to the base of an upright stone. It did not matter that we had brought nothing to dig with, for the ground was easy to pry up with our fingers. We placed the basket with the kitten in the hole then covered it with moss before returning the soil.

I had no wish to return to the mainland where we might meet with Myghal again. Instead, I showed the boy how to make boats of leaves, and we floated them down the crack in the rock to see them plunge into the pool. Judging by his laughter, the boy enjoyed our play, yet he did not appear completely at ease, and every so often, I would catch him looking up through the tall trees, as if to reassure himself there was still a sky up there.

"Why don't we go back down to the shore," I said, and took off at a run down the steep mountain side, leaping over fallen trees, ducking under low branches. The boy followed close on my heels, laughing all the way. We reached the bottom out of breath. While I sat upon the shore to rest, the boy stood with his face toward the sun. To me he was a sun as well, lit by some secret, inner joy. By contrast I felt myself dark, a creature of the night suddenly caught out in the light.

I have always believed we come into this world with a weight about our necks. We cannot see it, but it is there all the same. As children, we hardly notice it, but as the years pass, it gets heavier, until by the time we reach old age, our backs are bent, our legs bowed. This unseen weight weighs down our thoughts as well, especially when we wish to sleep. We toss and turn yet find no position where the weight does not press upon us. Years go by, and we cannot remember the last time we woke feeling refreshed.

Yet on that day, sitting in the sand and bathed in the boy's shining presence, I felt as light as one of the clouds drifting across the sky. Mind you, I do not wish to portray the boy as some fairy creature, all fluff and feathers, for there was a solemn side to him as well, when he would stare out across the water, looking sad. Yet this shadow soon passed, and laughing, he would run along the shore, kicking up the water in a great spray that split the light into the colors of the rainbow.

We discovered a way to learn about our people's different ways by making things in the sand. I made the houses of our village, using pebbles for the walls and bits of driftwood for the steep roofs. Small tunnels poked in the sand were the mines. The boy used only sand to make the houses of his people. They were square and flat-roofed, and some had windows atop windows. I shook my head over them, for such houses could never have withstood even one of our winter storms. To prove my point, I flung handfuls of sea water onto them, and we both watched as the little houses melted back into the sand.

When we grew hungry, we cracked open mussels and swallowed the meats raw. Then we played games that I suppose children everywhere play: tag, hide and seek, follow the leader, and all the while the two of us laughing like madmen. I don't believe I ever felt happier, and I said a prayer, asking the gods to make time stand still so that this day would never end. Yet when I finally stopped to catch my breath, I saw that the sun was already low in the west, which meant the sea had started its return, and here when the tide comes in, it comes on wings.

Fearing we had left it too late, I grabbed the boy's hand and ran with him to the channel where already the water was knee deep and rising. I stood there, wondering what to do. I dare not delay in returning the boy to his uncle. Yet I feared the strong current, for I am small and easily knocked about by the waves. Moreover, there were those places of sinking sand, now hidden by the water.

The boy did not share my fear and walked right out into the sea. I did not know if I should let him, since he had no experience of these waters. Yet when he turned and beckoned, I lifted up my skirt and followed. We got ourselves halfway across before a wave bigger than the rest knocked me down. I managed to stand back up, but my wet clothes were heavy upon me, and when another wave came, I could not lift myself above it and was knocked down again. As I tried to push up, one arm sank down into the sand. Then my whole body began to slip downward, as if I were on a talus slope and the ground rolling out from under me. In the trough behind the wave, I managed to get my head above water and saw the boy reaching out. With my free hand, I grabbed his, and he pulled me up out of the sinking sand. I was shaking from my icy drenching and from my fear of nearly being swallowed up. The boy tried to reassure me with a smile, but how could I be reassured by someone who did not know these waters as I did? Our best course was to return the way we came, and I tried to pull him back that direction, but he shook his head and pulled me forward. We were not long at our tug-of-war before another large wave struck. With the boy's help, I was able to rise with it, my shirt spreading out as I bobbed above the swell. When my feet touched down, the boy pulled me forward once more. This time I did not fight him, and with my ceasing to resist, the sea grew calm, and we reached the safety of the mainland where we found Myghal, pacing the shore and looking angrier than ever.

"Where the hell have you been?" he said. "Da's had me looking all over for you."

The way my teeth were chattering, I could not reply. Besides, what could I have said that would have appeased him? I gathered up my wet skirt, and we followed Myghal, trying to keep up with his long strides, for he seemed intent upon putting distance between himself and the boy and me. As we crested a dune, I saw Father and Talek talking to the boy's uncle near to where the blacks waited beside the boat. I feared Father would be angry, but as we drew near, I heard him laugh at something the boy's uncle said. This was a good sign, for it not only meant he was not angry, but that he had sold his tin as well.

The boy's uncle saw us and spoke sharply to the boy and gestured toward the boat. It was then sadness like another icy wave swept over me, for I realized the boy was leaving, likely never to return. As he had when we first met, he bowed. Then he took a pouch that hung by a cord from around his neck and pressed into my hand. I had no time to open it, for I was fumbling in the pocket of my skirt for the small blade I kept there. I used it to lop off a lock of my red hair, which I gave to him. He looked pleased. Then his uncle spoke sharply again, and the boy hopped into the boat, and the two blacks pushed it out into the water.

"So what did the little shit give you?" Myghal said, poking the pouch with a stiff finger.

"Never you mind," Father said. "Just you go and give Cador a good rubdown. You brought him back in a lather."

My father turned to me and smiled.

"You sell your tin, did you, Da?"

"Aye, that we did," he said, tossing and catching a bag heavy with coins. Then he threw an arm around Talek's shoulders, and off they went together, singing a tune.

I waited until they were out of sight before sitting down to examine my gift. I opened the pouch to find large grains of what looked like ordinary tree resin. But my disappointment turned to delight when I chanced to scratch one, thereby releasing a fragrance as perfumed as roses. I leapt up to yell my thanks, but, of course, the boy and his uncle were already far out to sea, almost to the large sail boat they came in.

Within a year of having sold his tin to the foreigners, Father took sick. It was the lung sickness. As he lay dying, he told Myghal to look after the mine, then out of Myghal's hearing, he told me to look after Myghal. "Try to keep him out of too much mischief, at least until such time as you're safely married." Then he told me how sad he was that he would not live to see that day.

Perhaps Myghal had been eavesdropping, for Father was barely in the ground when he told me I was not to marry until he gave his say so. I was not surprised by this, for it seemed every day Myghal grew more the tyrant. Yet I did not care, for I did not want a husband. In my mind, I was married already.

I did my best by Father's request, to look after Myghal, and got my share of cuffs for my pains. Then one day Myghal took it into his head to change one of the boundary ditches. Perhaps he thought no one would notice. More likely it was his wanting to pick a fight with Cadan, our neighbor, whose land bordered ours. Well, a fight is certainly what Myghal got, though not with the results he expected. While Myghal had Cadan down, beating his head into the hard ground, Cadan's son came up behind and bashed Myghal with a rock. They brought him to me unconscious, blood pouring from his mouth and ears. I was three months nursing him back to life, or to a half-life, for Myghal was never the same. Most of the strength was gone from one side of his body, forcing him to go about dragging one leg. His speech was also affected, and only I could understand him, and what a torment it was that his sister, whom he loved so little, now had to act as his interpreter. On his blackest days, he would rave and threaten to kill anyone that chanced to cross his path, though he was so weak all his threats got him was laughter. When that happened, he would drag himself home, curl up in a corner and cry. It was then I would take out my gift, the resin the boy gave me, take a grain and set it to burning in a bowl. Just a grain was enough to fill our little house with a sweet fragrance, which helped to calm Myghal.

We were ten years living like prisoners to each other, Myghal bound to me by his needs, and I to him by my father's dying request. Then one winter's night, as gale winds battered our house, Myghal died. I confess his death was a relief, though I cannot blame him for being as he was. As I said, we are born with a weight, and for Myghal, the weight was made heavier.

Yet I have come to learn there is a power that works against the weight, something that lifts us up even as we are weighed down. I am not saying we sprout piskie wings and flutter about all smiles and giggles, for there were times with Myghal when I lashed him with sharp words, when he struck me and I struck back, when he lay weeping and I refused him the comfort of the resin. I am not proud to have done these things, yet considering the torment he put me through, even as I tried to do all I could for him, I do not fault myself overly much.

So, what is this being lifted up, if not piskie wings? I can only think of it as a will, a determination to do what is right even when, for the life of me, I could not figure a reason why I should. I suppose you might call it goodness. Yet in all my time caring for Myghal, I never thought of myself as good. If I acted kindly, it was not because I was kind. That is what I mean by being lifted up. We are given a power to be greater than we are. Yet such power never brought me happiness, only an ability to endure.

After Myghal's death, I gathered up the few things I wished to take from my father's house then got Talek with his donkey cart to carry me and my belongings out to the Mount. It was something I had been wanting to do for a long time, to live away from the mainland with its sad memories. Yet I also had the memory of that happy day spent with the boy, and in moving to the Mount, I suppose I was trying to see if I could reclaim that happiness. Now that I have lived to be an old woman, I have come to know that happiness is not the be-all and end-all, for though happiness spices life, it is not the meat of it. Not to say I do not laugh, for I do, often for no reason. Yet happiness seems a thing not of me, but a songbird that comes and goes as it pleases, whereas the love I share lives and breathes within me.

How is it, you might ask, that an old woman who lives alone shares love? It is because each day I sense the presence of the boy beside me as I go about my tasks, though I no longer think him a boy, but a man, stout like his uncle with a beard to match. The eyes, however, are the same: bright with that secret joy that I could not name before, but now know to be love. His love fills me and is my constant companion, though how this can be I do not know, for I only knew the boy for a day, and that day nearly a lifetime ago. Yet some things are best not reasoned and should remain a mystery, for life is not diminished by mystery, but made richer, even by that mystery called death.

On a late winter's day, when the first daffodils appeared, poking their heads up through patches of snow, I was at the spring, the one where the boy and I floated our boats made of leaves. There I saw the water go from clear to blood red, and it stayed that way for a night, a day and another night. I tried to keep vigil, but it was a long time to stay awake, and just before dawn of the second morning, I fell asleep, and in sleeping had a dream wherein Myghal and I stood at a fork in the road where one branch led down to the sea while the other went up over the headlands toward Uncle Jory's farm. Though in waking life we knew that fork well, in my dream Myghal and I stood there, thinking ourselves lost. I was of the opinion we should follow the road toward the sea, whereas Myghal, being his old devil self, argued for the road toward Uncle Jory's. Yet just to look that direction filled me with dread. When I refused to follow Myghal, he knocked me down then stood over me, cursing.

Now, here is the really odd thing, for in addition to there being a split in the road, I sensed there was a split within each of us as well. Even as Myghal stood over me, cursing, I saw that one part of him was good, for despite of all I have said about Myghal, there was goodness in him. Yet the gods cursed him with a terrible pride, and goodness never won out when his pride was at stake.

Perhaps the gods cursed me as well, though rather than pride, they gave me an open heart. I think back to that day when Myghal killed that poor kitten. Why did it trouble me so? Why does any cruelty bring me sorrow? It is because there is a window into my heart, and the pain others feel passes through it so that I feel it also. I cannot count the number times I have wanted to shutter that window to keep out the pain, and perhaps I could have, for I do not believe that what we are given, what makes us who we are, is something we ourselves cannot change, and having suffered the pain of an open heart, I would not fault another were she to shutter the heart's window to keep the pain out.

Yet pain is only part of what passes through my window. It lets in love and affection as well. Moreover, it freely allows these gifts to pass both ways, for I would be a cursed indeed were I able to receive love yet not give it in return, even when another part of me sometimes does not wish to.

And what is that other part, that half of the split within me? Surely it is not one thing, but many: stubbornness, willfulness, spite, envy, laziness and a good handful of nearly every other evil I can think of. But mostly it is fear, the worst vice of all, for how much more love could I have shared had I not been afraid?

The sun coming up over the mainland woke me from my dream. At once, I saw that the spring was running clear once more. Clear in my mind also was the knowledge that the boy I played with that day so long ago was now dead. I grieved for the loss of the one I had been married to in spirit, yet was given some comfort in knowing that no matter how much he might have suffered in death, he was beyond suffering now. Yet part of him lived in the love I still felt for him, which made me realize that love is not something that passes from this world when we do.

A robin landed on a rock not more than an arm's length away. I watched until she had finished taking a bath in the pool then I stood up and began to gather stones, for I had decided I would build a shrine about the spring.

I am still building it. Likely, I shall never finish, for the stones are heavy, and I am far from young. Yet by doing this, I am keeping the memory of the boy alive. The work also allows me time to think, and often I find myself returning to that part of my dream wherein Myghal and I stood arguing about which fork in the road to take. I believe the dream was telling me that in this world, even though we know the landmarks, we are lost.

So how do we find ourselves? Perhaps in the choices we make, the roads we choose to follow. Yet I am certain that, on my own, I was not wise enough to make the right choices, not without a guide, someone who was there when I needed help finding my way.

I have already told how the boy saved me from drowning, and how, with my hand in his, the sea grew calm. What I did not say was that when my feet touched down, it was not upon the ocean floor, but upon the surface of the water, which somehow the boy had made as solid as rock. At first, I was afraid as anyone would be, doing that which defies nature. But the boy's smile reassured me. From my high place atop the water, I could see Myghal standing upon the far shore. I could tell that he either did not, or could not, see us walking upon the water. I have never understood why I, alone, was a witness to this miracle. Perhaps we do not find our way by making choices after all; we find our way because we are chosen.

O, Myghal, would our lives have been different if you had been the one walking upon the water as I stood there upon the shore? Would the sheer wonder of it have humbled your pride? Why it is you were given to self-hate, while I was chosen to stand upon the water as from the boy's hand love filled me like sunlight flooding the world?

Made in the USA
Las Vegas, NV
02 December 2021